8/20/12

Between
You & Me

Between You & Me

Marisa Calin

BLOOMSBURY

NEW YORK LONDON NEW DELHI SYDNEY

First published in the United States of America in August 2012
by Bloomsbury Books for Young Readers
www.bloomsburyteens.com

For information about permission to reproduce selections from this book, write to
Permissions, Bloomsbury BFYR, 175 Fifth Avenue, New York, New York 10010

Library of Congress Cataloging-in-Publication Data
Calin, Marisa.
Between you & me / by Marisa Calin. — 1st U.S. ed.
p. cm.
Summary: Phyre, sixteen, narrates her life as if it were a film, capturing her crush on Mia, a student teacher of theater and film studies, as well as her fast friendship with a classmate referred to only as "you."
ISBN 978-1-59990-758-1
[1. Interpersonal relations—Fiction. 2. Student teachers—Fiction. 3. Teachers—Fiction. 4. Theater—Fiction. 5. Acting—Technique—Fiction. 6. High schools—Fiction. 7. Schools—Fiction. 8. Love—Fiction.] I. Title. II. Title: Between you and me.
PZ7.C12868Bet 2012 [Fic]—dc23 2011035066

Book design by Regina Roff
Typeset by Westchester Book Composition
Printed in the U.S.A. by Quad/Graphics, Fairfield, Pennsylvania
2 4 6 8 10 9 7 5 3 1

All papers used by Bloomsbury Publishing, Inc., are natural, recyclable products made from wood grown in well-managed forests. The manufacturing processes conform to the environmental regulations of the country of origin.

To the incomparable B. Bowen
And the divine M. Miller

Between You & Me

FADE IN

MY BEDROOM. SEPTEMBER. EVENING.

CLOSE-UP. HEART-SHAPED PINK SUNGLASSES. HIDING A FACE. MUSIC PLAYS. THE SUN FALLS ACROSS THE BEDROOM IN A BRIGHT SHAFT OF LIGHT. CUT TO: WIDE SHOT. GIRL LIES ON HER BED, PROPPED ON HER ELBOWS, CHIN IN HER HANDS.

Phyre, sixteen, that's me! And this is my life. Or how I picture it. The door swings open and I smile up at you.

ME

Come in. Close the door behind you.

We painted my name on it when we were seven. *Phyre,* still there because we used oil paint and nothing covers it. Put regular paint on top and it beads and wipes right off, like watercolor on wax crayon. Purple, because it's my favorite color, the color of this bedroom! Depending on the light. See how everything burns pink in the sun?

ME

Sit down!

I swing a hand toward your usual spot.

YOU

Stylish sunnies, Phy!

The sunglasses were a present from you, a joke, but I wear them anyway. I slide them down my nose, then fling them at you, shielding my eyes from the sun as you catch them and sink into my beanbag. I laugh at your serious face as you put them on. Nice new jeans, I see, watching you jam your hands into your pockets and cross your ankles out in front of you. They look good on you. We're not the kids that started in first grade together, I think, smiling at the ridiculous pink heart reflections cast across your cheek.

I roll onto my back, resting my head on my hands, and gaze out the window. The trees are already turning to a fiery gold, the sun dipping behind them as I watch. A gust of wind sends yellow leaves falling like rain. I look at you over the top of my head, a shadow dividing your upside-down face in two. You push the sunglasses up into your fair hair so I can see every shade of your green eyes.

YOU

Can you believe it's the first day of school tomorrow?

I shake my head, catching sight of the outfit I've laid out. I squeeze my eyes shut and spread my arms across the bed. I haven't been nervous for a first day since we were five and I saw you sitting in the classroom refusing to take off your backpack. I'm lucky to start every new year with you.

. . . . . .

SCHOOL HALLWAY. MONDAY MORNING. FIRST DAY.

We ride the wave of the hallway, returning familiar smiles. Everyone has the glow of summer about them. I tuck a rogue strand of brown hair behind my ear, the fire-engine red growing out of my bangs so it looks like just the tips are on fire. I wave at Cara. She looks very *Vogue* in stripes and skinny black jeans, her dark hair cropped to her chin this year.

CARA

Phyre Power!

Cara wants to make movies too, and smiles at me with the casual scrutiny she looks at the world with, like someone watching a story piece itself together in pictures.

CARA

Good summer?

The question ripples between people down the hall as she gives me a salute and we roll on.

Kate heads toward us and asks you if you're signed up for swimming. You've been on the team for the last couple of years. A few more greetings are sent your way and I spare you a sideways glance. You're getting more and more attention every year—growing into your good looks, my mom called it. I elbow you fondly, wondering whether I'll have to remind you who was there for you when you were awkward looking.

. . . . . .

SUNNY CLASSROOM. THAT AFTERNOON.

Curled forward in my chair, I'm filling in my timetable on the inside cover of my notebook. My mouth has slid into its pout—my concentrating face, you call it. We get to take a theater and film class this year, so I'm excited, and there's a student teacher for the first semester, which is theater studies. We're sitting in haphazard rows; class hasn't started. Ryan is sitting on Bella's desk, knees wide apart like boys do, inviting her to a party that will probably end up as a party of two. He's an attention seeker. He can make you feel special one on one, but in front of people he has something to prove. Trust me, we went out for a few weeks last year. Sitting on the windowsill, I can see you frowning from here. He's not your favorite person—you've never been the kind to fool around.

Tony, Ryan's sidekick, taps me on the shoulder and rocks forward.

TONY

Hey.

He rests his forearm across the back of my chair.

So.

I raise an encouraging eyebrow.

How's it going?

And it's thanks to this firecracker opener that when the door opens I'm slow to look around.

She stands in the square of sun from the window, and a rainbow of colors from the prism hanging on the latch dance across her face. She steps forward so that they flicker against her shoulder instead. I sit, watching her, forgetting Tony hovering behind me. There's something about her, something fascinating. You can't cast someone to be fascinating, they just are. She's young, warm. All eyes are on her as she unwinds a cream scarf and drapes it over the back of her chair. She looks up:

MIA

My name is Miss Quin.

She smiles.

You can call me Mia.

She smooths her hand over the base of her chestnut bob to tame the static from her scarf, wisps of hair still flaring away from her neck. She steps out from behind her desk, perching against it, not separating herself from us like most teachers. I sit up straighter. Her voice is rich, engaging.

MIA

The moment you step out onstage, people start forming an impression of you. Just as you're already forming an impression of me.

She looks at each of us with crystal-cool blue eyes, the warmest cool you've ever seen, like water in the sun.

MIA

And you're already telling me something about yourselves.

Self-conscious, I swallow and ease back in my chair so as not to seem too keen. She sees me, and asks my name. "Phyre" sounds louder than I expected, embarrassingly so, like flames are leaping and I'm the first to notice. She smiles.

MIA

Phyre here seems ready to learn something new.

She looks at Ryan, rocked back on his chair, his arms folded across his chest. She gestures for his name, which he volunteers with emphasis.

MIA

Ryan, it seems, thinks he might have better things to do!

People laugh. She crosses her arms like him and, embarrassed, he tips back farther, then flails with that falling sensation and comes back onto four legs with a bump. He blushes and looks at the floor. He clearly thinks she's hot, which is probably why he's trying to play it cool. She lightens up.

MIA

Maybe he just wants us to think he has better things to do. Either way, physical life is a key element when creating a character onstage.

Mia walks between the desks, crisp and perfect, her white shirt tucked seamlessly into a high-waisted navy skirt. My shirt is lily pink with white pinstripes that flutter as I look at them. Compared to her, I look like I slept in my shirt, then rolled to school. She adjusts her collar as she passes me. I smell something sweet like lavender.

MIA

So! Let's get to know each other.

She slides back onto her desk, crossing slim ankles that swing gently as she picks up the class list, pressing her pen tip to the first name. I glance quickly around the room. Everyone else seems the same as ever. Elle, in the first row, pouting under blond bangs, is arranging the ribbon at the waist of her yellow top. She always looks glazed but usually turns out to have been listening, and—case in point—her hand goes up when Mia calls her name. Eva, beside her, the picture of concentration, perfects her hair clips for her turn. She has a prissy expression but I think it's the natural arrangement for her face. Mia is looking up brightly to memorize each of us. Kate meets her gaze attentively. Good at everything and intimidating in the chameleon-like way she fits into every group, Kate somehow manages to seem equally interested in everything.

Mia calls my name. She already knows who I am but for some reason my heart picks up pace when she looks at me.

MIA

Phyre. Great name!

—Rhetorical maybe but here's my chance to shine graciously. Still thinking . . . something clever on the tip of my tongue . . . and she's moved on! I turn to see you smiling at me. I can't hide much from you, which is a mixed blessing, but I'm usually never tongue-tied, so I guess you've noticed. I glare at you halfheartedly as Mia calls your name. You return her nod warmly and for the second time today I see how comfortable you're getting with everyone.

Bella, amid a circle of boys behind me, raises a hand for her name. She's "hot," honey-hued curly hair loosely pinned up, looking casually perfect with no apparent effort, as if she spent no time achieving *perfectness.* To make matters worse: she's nice. Ryan, next to her, has regained his confidence and is whipping Tony with his ruler. Most people think Ryan's good-looking, which makes him even less bearable—and, worse still, he *is,* so there are grounds to be cocky. I see glimmers in his eyes of the true him, someone real and scared, and then I like him for a second, until he speaks. Tony catches my eye again. At first glance he veers toward scruffy but I think he's effortfully disheveled. I've seen him look quite neat until he sees his reflection and tugs his shirt out of his pants. He'd be better off if he didn't traipse around after Ryan, so that's probably his greatest flaw, but then high school compromises people's abilities to think for themselves.

Cara brings me back with her cheerful greeting when Mia calls her name. Her greatest talent is to seem impervious to peer pressure, which means she is—she's on her own raft of cool. Reaching the end of the list, Mia sets it down beside her.

MIA

First things first! To be real, you have to know yourself and your reactions. We're looking for truth, and to find truth we need trust. That's where we'll start. Trust.

She looks around the room and smiles conspiratorially.

We need space. Follow me!

And as she hops off the desk, I glimpse someone who's not just an adult suspended in circumstance but a person, with a childhood, a life, her own reality. She isn't hiding. We can see her figure, the way she moves.

. . . . . .

PLAYING FIELDS. SOON AFTER.

The sun is warm, bathing the playing fields in golden light. There is grass beneath our feet, and the smell of wet leaves.

We felt rebellious stealing through the deserted halls during class. Mia claps her hands together, more with excitement than authority. Her shirt still has the perfect unrumpled tuck even when she pushes up her sleeves, the white fabric luminescent in the light.

MIA

Okay. Pair up and spread out in two lines facing each other.

We pair up with a glance and you head to one side of the field as I go to the other. Squinting in the glow of sun, I can see the fuzzy haze of my own eyelashes. Mia gestures to my row, calling across the grass.

MIA

This side, close your eyes, and run toward your partner.

I hear some laughs ring out but she's serious, so I close my eyes tentatively, my eyelids flickering. It's hard to close your eyes when you're so awake. I'm in a world of her voice.

MIA

Give yourself to the moment. Feel the ground under your feet. You can't think about falling. Just think about running.

With just the pinkish black of my eyelids to look at, everything moves slower. I take a step. My mind puts bars around me that root me to the spot. There's nothing near, I tell myself, not even a shadow, and I can hear your voice calling. So with my eyes squeezed tight shut, I run. Really run! My other senses feel stronger. I hear my name alone on the sound waves. Sometimes the ground falls away, and I stumble but stay on my feet and keep running. I must look like a crazed three-year-old, my steps short and knees so high. Your voice gets closer and closer until I feel the jarring of your hands on my shoulders and open my eyes to see you and, beside you, Mia.

MIA

Good, Phyre. *Excellent!*

This is where it starts, the very beginning.

. . . . . .

PEELE'S. LATE AFTERNOON.

We're in town, in Peele's, *The coffee shop on the corner*, as it says in reverse lettering on the glass beside us. School ended a few hours ago but I didn't feel like going home. We're at our favorite window table, peering out into the street. It's warm and cozy in here; outside, the street looks steeped in blue. I can smell autumn in the air and I'm wearing a scarf for the first time this fall. I tug my pink cuffs over my hands and wrap my palms around my mug, sliding an elbow across the copper tabletop so I can get a better view, beneath *corner*, of Elle and Jen crossing the street. You take a sip of hot chocolate and run your fingers through your sun-lightened hair, a gesture I'd know a mile away.

YOU

Summer has changed people, don't you think? This year feels different—

A figure sweeps by the window, a figure I recognize.

ME

There's Mia!

I'm sure that's her, in the plum-colored jacket with the collar turned up. Something in me wants her to turn and see me but as I rub away the mist from my breath on the window that separates us from the world, she disappears into the bookstore on the corner. I could go after her, casually bump into her. It's strangely tempting, the idea of seeing her in this world beyond school. I turn to say so but the waitress appears with my smiling pumpkin cookie, and my chance is lost.

My cookie stares up at me, its smile mocking me. One of its icing-eyes was smudged in the making and it looks like it's winking. I pick it off and suck the icing from my finger. You're talking about who's already got together this year. I watch you stir your hot chocolate and do the same. It's starting to feel too warm in here and I'm grateful for the cool air that spills in each time the door swings open. You catch my eye and smile, reviving my attempts to give you my full attention. It's a good thing I didn't go tearing down the street after Mia. I sit back in my seat, trying to feel glad I stayed, but my eyes flitter back and forth till the light begins to fade and the glass starts to show a reflection of myself.

. . . . . .

THE STREET. SOON AFTER.

In the crisp air, Peele's glowing windows behind us, I can't help glancing hopefully into the bookstore. It's been nearly an hour but something still stops me from walking straight past. I swing around the awning in the doorway for a better look and the perfect excuse comes to me.

ME

Did you see the reading list for English? There are a couple of things I don't have. Wanna take a look?

I try for an indifferent nod toward the bookstore and you smile obligingly and follow me in without seeming to give it a thought.

■ ■ ■ ■ ■

THE BOOKSTORE. MOMENTS LATER.

We walk the shelves at the perimeter of the store but I don't see even a glimpse of Mia's plum-clad figure. *Get a grip, Phyre.* I shake myself. She wouldn't still be here, she has better things to do than live in the bookstore! I scoop up a few books as my interest in pretending to shop vanishes and head straight to the register. You meander behind, flicking through books, actually interested, actually in the moment. I wish I didn't feel as strangely distracted as I have all day. You reach the counter and buy something—from the glimpse I get, not a school text, but a book on cinema, which is weird; it's more my thing. We head back into the evening air.

■ ■ ■ ■ ■

THE STREET. EARLY EVENING.

I look up into the navy blue twilight sky and skip ahead of you, trying to shake this feeling, wondering why it even mattered to me if Mia was still there. Tugging my sweater on, I turn to you with a busy smile.

ME

Hey, so, do you like anyone this year?

You shrug and tap your toe in a puddle, sending a ripple out to the edges, your hands wedged into your pockets as always. All of a sudden, you have my complete attention.

ME

You do! I can tell!

I swing at your arm.

YOU

Huh?

You heard me, I know, and I can see you smiling as you turn away.

ME

Come on! Tell me. I tell you everything!

You shrug again, evasively, but, despite another playful shove, give nothing else away, and tuck your chin in as we turn toward my house.

. . . . . .

MY BEDROOM. SOON AFTER.

Stretched out on my bed, you've avoided any further conversation about romantic interests. I'm curled on the window seat, waving a pen with a pink streamer on the end, and not taking no for an answer:

ME

There *is* someone, isn't there? You have a crush!

A harmless crush? Right? The topic is unusually interesting to me today. I can't see your face but I fling a pillow at you, which you catch with great satisfaction.

YOU

Quick like a cat!

I shake my head despairingly and take the moment to casually mention Mia, that I think she's cool. Relieved—probably that I'm no longer badgering you—you perk up and roll onto your front.

YOU

Yeah, she seems nice.

Mm-hmm is my super-dynamic reply as you flip open the computer. I'm not a big social surfer but curiosity wins out now and again, and I hop onto the bed beside you. We scroll past the school hot list, which I made an appearance on last year but just for a week, and I'm glad not to feature on any scandal lists. Then there are the gossip pages but we spend all day at school so I don't see the need to talk about it online in the evening. This time, though, I punch Mia's name into the search to see if anyone has mentioned her. Three hits since this afternoon, including *Check out the new hottie.* I flip the computer shut and slide up the volume on the song playing. *Secret heart.* I sit up again quickly and peer suspiciously at my play list. *This very secret that you're trying to conceal/Is the very same one that you're dying to reveal.* This has been a strange day. When I see you looking at me, I say something about the crap people post with a noise that was supposed to be blasé but sounded possessed. My abruptness is fortunately eclipsed by the cat coming into the room and hopping up onto the bed with a purr. She pushes her head into the palm of your hand, giving me a moment to wonder what it is about some people, and why I should feel protective of a person I hardly know. Holly (Golightly) flops onto her back and I watch you stir her tabby fur, remembering the day she first came home and we let her squirm in our cupped hands.

You check the time. Nearly 8:00.

YOU

Crap. Gotta go!

You grab your shoes.

ME

Time flies when you're with me . . .

You zip your smile into the neck of your hoodie. You're busy this year, always something to do. I'm not sure I like it. We used to hang out for hours.

ME

What's tonight? Karate?

You nod, heading to the door. I came with you to a few classes last year. I had dreams of being a spy—martial arts an obvious prerequisite—but there's a lot of stretching and you get pink and sweaty. I realized that what I actually want is to be a spy in movies where there is never pinkness or sweat. So you could say that I want to be an actress. I hand you your stack of books at the door.

YOU

See you tomorrow.

You salute and bound downstairs.

......

SCHOOL THEATER. TUESDAY AFTERNOON.

We're here for our first real class with Mia. As I gaze at the arch that sweeps above the stage and at the lights on the deep plum curtains drawn closed, the theater feels alive, full of expectation. It's exciting to walk down the aisle, sidestepping into a row of seats. Mia sits at the front of the stage in a circle of light.

MIA

Purpose.

I sit forward to be closer.

Everything we do is the pursuit of an objective. Some are fulfilled in seconds, some take a lifetime, but there's a reason for every action, so let that purpose propel you from one moment to the next.

She takes an orange from her pocket.

Remember how it felt running with your eyes closed? You had to be in the moment.

She throws the orange unexpectedly to Kate in the second row. Kate's hand shoots out to catch it, startling her and making Mia laugh.

MIA

Excellent! Be receptive to your impulses.

Kate throws it back, Mia smiling, engaged.

See how you're all now rooted in this moment.

She pretends to throw it a few times before sending it toward Tony. She smiles again and so do I.

Your intention to catch the orange triggered your response to reach out.

He returns the throw and she tucks the orange back in her pocket.

You wouldn't catch an orange that no one threw. That would be weird! Keep that in mind onstage so you're never speaking or moving without a reason.

Stand up because you need to. No pacing, no musical chairs or hugging furniture. And no crazy gesturing.

I laugh so much at her demonstration that some people stare. My post-laugh sigh is still tapering off as she disappears into the wings. After a moment, the curtains open and we're looking at a single desk and chair center stage, exactly the same as the ones in any classroom. Mia reappears.

MIA

First, you're just going to be you. Let's get past any self-consciousness and the thought of being watched. Put a fourth wall between yourself and the audience. I'd like you each to come up and spend two minutes onstage, as if you were by yourself. Sounds easy enough, right?

She presses her hands together.

Imagine you're the first into class. Arrive exactly as you would. Create the classroom in your mind and try to believe that you have two minutes alone at your desk before anyone else comes in. Engage with a task you would realistically be doing.

She smiles, running her eyes around the room with a curious smile.

Anyone like to go first?

A quiet pause. I don't see the hand go up behind me.

Eva! That's what I like to see.

Eva? *Crap. Should have volunteered.* She stands up and smooths out her skirt. I never had her pegged as an actress type, which goes to show I shouldn't peg. Clutching her bag, she makes her way toward the stage. Mia moves to a seat in the first row, her elegant chin raised, gazing up at her.

MIA

Think about where you've just come from. Close your eyes and experience the hall in your mind before you step into the classroom. We need to get the impression we're seeing a snippet of a seamless existence.

Eva nods and amid a few hushed whispers heads behind the curtain. My stomach flutters, nervous for my turn. She takes her time and when she finally reappears, she's herself. I'm impressed how familiar it seems, watching her carefully unpack her books neatly on the desk and tuck her bag beneath it the way I see her do every day. She seems to accept exactly who she is, embracing the traits that people make fun of, and I feel a pang of fondness for her. She opens her book for English, smooths flat her ribbon bookmark, and then she reads. Just reads, her expression a genuine pout of concentration. Two minutes are over so quickly. She looks up expectantly when Mia speaks.

MIA

Very good, Eva. You came into the room with very believable purpose. Great work.

Eva beams, her usual prissy expression falling back into place as she returns to her seat. Mia looks thoughtfully at the class, scrunching up her nose in a way that I know I will come to love. I watch her eyes roll past me and my hand goes up before I've given it any thought. She returns her gaze to me and nods for me to come forward. Nerves pervade my chest as I grab my bag and climb past her onto the stage. She smiles at me. *Same thing,* she says.

Backstage, I take a breath. *Be natural,* I tell myself, gazing unseeingly at the ripples in the curtain. *Try not to think of Mia.* Given that for some reason I've been thinking of her since she arrived, it would be true of this moment for her to be on my mind. So I close my eyes and, picturing the hallway outside her classroom, the smell, the blue notice board with the paper peeling up in the corner, I push through my imagined door, stepping out onstage. No one here yet. Mia's jacket on the back of her chair. Maybe she'll be the first to arrive. I swing my bag onto my desk, then check the glass square in the door for any sign of her. I'm rearranging my bangs in the hazy shape of my reflection there when I realize I never finished copying my timetable into my notebook. I sit down and take out the book and a pen. I've reached Wednesday. No Mia Wednesday, the dark day. Thursday starts with Mia and we have her Monday and Tuesday afternoons. Friday I can get through. Theater is what I want to be good at, three periods a week to win her respect. Maybe I care too much about what people think? But no more than anyone else, right? Everyone cares, that's how we measure success—by what people think. I fill in Thursday. So it's normal that I sometimes say what I think I should say, hide what I think I should hide. I push my hair back from my forehead again, absentmindedly twirling it around my finger and wondering for a second how people see me, whether it's anything like how I see myself.

MIA

Excellent!

I look up, seeing the room full of eyes on me. I embraced my real-life thoughts, gave myself to the moment. I gaze at Mia's open expression, her involved eyes. She nods, and my heart is still racing as I settle again beside you.

Ryan is next. He puts his head on his desk and sleeps for two minutes. Surprisingly believable. You can't quibble with the truth in that. Mia laughs. I make it my goal to elicit that perfect sound from her.

When the bell rings at the end of class, people collect together their things in an instant and flock toward the doors. I hang back, reaching underneath the seat for my bag. Mia is still at the front of the stage, so I wave that I'll catch you up. I'm hoping to see her for a minute, and I'm thinking of a reason to speak to her. I've reached the stage—everyone else is leaving and Mia is following! I have to say something, to hold her back . . . I swallow. The words aren't coming. She's gone. Missed my chance.

. . . . .

HALLWAY. LATER THAT AFTERNOON.

Heading to the final class of the day, with a pang of excitement I see Mia leaving her room and coming toward me. With the hallway emptying, here's a chance to make up for earlier! My heart beats faster. I look casually at the notice boards lining the walls until I'm ready to make eye contact. She's adjusting the shoulder of her ruched purple shirt. We're about to pass, I have this one moment to speak. We draw even, she looks up and smiles.

ME

Hi—

She returns the greeting expectantly, smiling for another moment—and we continue on our way! My tone seems to hang in the air as I stare blankly down the hall. It sounded like a question, like I was going to go on, a precursor to something interesting, but there it stayed. Embarrassingly incomplete. Somehow, she even compromises my ability to say hello right! This has never happened to me before. I've never been shy to talk to anyone. I used to ask our sexy history teacher to write *everything* on the board so we could whoop at his sculpted butt when he turned around. But this? It's all I can do to stop from banging my head against the wall. As I head into English, I try to convince myself of the possibility that she thinks I'm intriguingly enigmatic, and not a moron.

▪ ▪ ▪ ▪ ▪

SCHOOL STEPS. AFTER SCHOOL. THE NEXT DAY.

In front of school, I'm sitting pigeon-toed with my chin on my knees, gazing at my shoes. You're a step down, probably a second away from smacking me on the head and telling me to snap out of it. I know I'm not the best company right now but at least I'm not regaling you with my conquests like

Grace, a girl in our year, three steps down. Apparently, she thinks Mr. Marsden, the new art teacher, is *smoking* hot. Me? I feel blue. This new feeling is depressing. Every time I see Mia, I can feel myself slipping further into my admiration of her. I should dig in my heels, make it stop. Maybe I'll just head home and shake it off. A hand on my thigh, and I'm sandwiched between Ryan and Tony. I can think of a lot of places I'd rather be sandwiched. Like between a rock and a hard place. It's Ryan's hand on my thigh. I sweep it off like a crumb.

RYAN

Hey, Phyre. You look hot.

I can never tell a real compliment from sparkling humor so I make a face. Ryan keeps going.

How can a hot girl like you be such an
ice queen?

ME

(Rising silently above it)

RYAN

Give Tony a chance. He likes you.

I turn to Tony. His knee has come through his jeans so the bottom of his pant leg is hanging on by a thread. He'd look stupid if it fell off. Stupid and cool are linked by a thread!

ME

Can you give me a good reason to go out with you?

This takes Tony by surprise. You're smiling, bouncing your eyes back and forth between us as he puzzles this one out. He's as good-looking as any guy in the year, better than most, but if he can't look me in the eye and make me feel something, then what's the point? Right? I pull at the rip in his jeans with my finger, shaking my head with playful disapproval.

ME

Care about yourself and people will care about you!

A home ec joke, and a quote from Mrs. Kook, our home ec teacher. Kook is not her real name but it's the only one I've ever called her. Everyone laughs, even Tony, but I can tell I embarrassed him. I wonder for a second why I'm being mean. I gaze past him and, with a leap of my heart, see Mia leaving school. I stand up impulsively.

ME

It's been fun, guys, but I have things to do.

Ryan is leaning back on the step like I may find him too irresistible to leave. I'll manage. I swing my bag over my shoulder and give you a look to say that you can come if you like. In a few steps you catch up and start walking with me toward the gate.

YOU

Heading home, or you wanna go through town?

I look over at Mia again, mid-conversation with *smoking* hot Mr. Marsden ahead of us. I want her to notice me—I can't explain it. With guys it's easy. You learn to expect what everyone else wants: hand holding, kissing, a sweet note to make you feel special. But feeling like this? And with a girl? I rub my forehead. I'll try not to think about it and maybe it'll go away. Mia has paused at the gate so we reach her and Mr. Marsden at the same time as Grace and a group of girls appear behind us. Their flirty attention on Mr. Marsden, we have the chance to say hi to Mia. This "hi" makes me sound perkier than a summer camp counselor. I take a vow of silence in my head. Ryan and Tony have caught up. I grab your sleeve and skirt to the edge of the pack to steer clear of association with gems like:

GRACE

Mr. Marsden, do you have a girlfriend?

Grace leans a forearm coyly on her friend Ginny's shoulder like she's a prop. If I were Ginny, I'd step away. Mia smiles as she gets the same inappropriate questioning. Her furtive raised eyebrow to whether she has a boyfriend seems like a yes—of course she does, it'd be crazy if she didn't. Having someone around like Grace, who says everything you would *never* dream of saying, has its perks. You can roll your eyes and still hear the answer. She persists.

GRACE

Do you live together?

Everyone seems to move in closer, reminding me of last year's French exchange group with their relaxed sense of personal space. Mia is squeezed out of view as more people flock through the gate. I feel like a toddler at a rock concert. You've said something but I'm still trying to hear her. Your voice again:

YOU

Phy? You coming?

When I reluctantly step away, I think I hear Ryan chiming in.

RYAN

Tony wants to know your position on dating students.

A fit of laughter. I glance back but from what I can see Mia is still smiling good-naturedly. We stop at the corner and I realize how much I wish I wanted to fawn all over Mr. Marsden.

YOU

You okay?

ME

Sure! Fine!

The answer is not *Sure! Fine!* so I'm not sure why I say it is. And you're not stupid, I know you don't believe me. I should have been honest—I'm always honest with you! But somehow this is different. I can't say anything yet, I can't define it and I'm not sure I want to. Seeing my focus shift over your shoulder again, you try for a sympathetic nod but I can see that you're feeling shut out.

YOU

So I'll see you tomorrow?

I return the nod and watch you take a couple of steps backward before you shift your bag onto your shoulder and swing away from me as we go our separate ways.

. . . . . .

MY BEDROOM. ALMOST MIDNIGHT.

Staring at the ceiling, I push the covers down, pulling a pillow into my arms and burying my face beneath it to shut out the shaft of moonlight from the gap in the curtains. My decision not to think about Mia is like deciding not to think about a pink elephant when someone says *Don't think about a pink elephant.* And, after all, there's nothing wrong with how I feel, right? It probably doesn't mean anything . . . Something Mom once said runs through my head: *Belonging is a privilege.* I take a ponderous breath and roll onto my back, pushing off the covers. Well, I think I took belonging for granted. At least, I don't want to be set apart. Not for this. I need to fit in.

Fifteen minutes later, I'm still staring at the ceiling. I think the angry purple is keeping me awake. It's always been my favorite color so I never gave it any thought but I suddenly feel like I can't have it there another minute. I untangle my feet from the sheet. Mom has aquamarine leftover from the spare room. I feel for the phone and call you on your cell as it's the middle of the night. The ringing sounds so loud in the darkness. You're on the end of the phone, sleepy, and maybe cross, I can't quite tell.

ME

Hi, it's me. Are you asleep?

YOU

Hmm?

ME

Can you come over and help me paint
my room?

YOU

Hmm? It'sthemiddleofthenight.

ME

I know, but purple isn't peaceful.

. . . . .

FRONT DOOR. SOON AFTER.

Whether you've come because you're the best friend anyone could ever have, or because you think I'm crazy and in need of help, you're on the front step and I love you. I pull open the door and stand there grinning at you. Can you see me through your bleary eyes? You're wearing pajama pants, a coat, and boots. If anyone could see you now they would understand friendship. We tiptoe upstairs. I'm clutching a can of paint.

. . . . .

MY BEDROOM. MINUTES LATER.

We can't listen to music like in movies because we'll wake Mom, so we paint in the silence of night. And standing here, brush in my hand, I recognize the true absurdity of this. You look my way and I shrug with a little grin. You give me your only-you smile, the one I get on these special occasions, and I know I'll always have you.

. . . . .

CUT TO: AN HOUR LATER.

Half the bedroom is painted. There's a green smear on your cheek from where you pushed your hair out of your eyes. The aquamarine hasn't quite covered the purple. That would take an undercoat or second coat so I shall consider it a special effect. The bottom of the sea in purple shadow.

. . . . .

SCHOOL COURTYARD. THURSDAY MORNING. THE NEXT WEEK.

It's a sunny morning and the golden brick of the school glows warmly. We cut across to the English rooms, and I catch my reflection in the window. I feel grown-up today, wearing new jeans and a purple V-neck that makes my boobs look good. You've commented, said, with a little smile of approval, that I look pretty, but you haven't asked why I'm dressing up these days. The remnants of red have been trimmed out of my hair but the sun intensifies my natural brown and I've started putting it up, which makes me look older. We have a class with Mia this morning, giving me a reason to make an effort. I hug my books to my chest and glance around as we continue to skirt the courtyard. You ask if I'm looking for Mia. I falter. Have I talked about her that much? I didn't think you'd noticed. Am I looking for her? Yes. Thinking about her? Have I stopped? I wonder if anyone notices me the way I notice her. I wonder if they *will* me to look toward them the way I hope with each step that she'll be around the next corner. I find myself waiting in places that I know she will be and, when I don't expect her, I look anyway. I know I'm blushing. And you're still waiting for an answer:

ME

For who? Mia? Oh, you know . . .

I have no idea what that's supposed to mean. I'm sure you don't either but you tactfully let it go. I see her then, in the reflection of the glass door as I pull it open, her sleek beautiful profile behind me. She's in a sky-blue shirt trimmed with lace, her hair pinned up. She looks almost like a schoolteacher today, the kind that shakes her hair loose under a waterfall in a shampoo commercial. For a minute we're framed together as people move through the door in the other direction. I see my reflection with hers there behind me, our images side by side. Next to her, my feeling of being grown-up evaporates instantly. She's so graceful—beside her I feel young, childish. I prefer the image I have of myself in my head to seeing us here together where I am small and unexceptional. Deflated, I follow you through the door into the frenzy of the voices and faces. It takes me a second to adjust and, as we move through the crowd, I press forward to reach the peace of the theater, not just because of Mia, but because the only thing that gives me pleasure besides being near her is her class.

▪ ▪ ▪ ▪ ▪ ▪

THEATER. SOON AFTER.

Mia comes down the aisle behind us, talking attentively to Kate, and passing us as we slide into a row of seats. Settling herself at the front, she clears her voice and raises her radiant eyes to us.

MIA

Sense memory!

Her expression invites input.

RYAN

The recall of physical sensation.

She rises above his choice of tone.

MIA

Correct! Remember, we visualize something every time we speak. Every thought triggers infinite images and associations.

She gestures to her necklace, playing with the delicate silver pendant. I look at her hands. They're soft and narrow.

MIA

Every little thing contains a sequence of memories—where it came from, what it means to you. Characters need those to feel real onstage.

She catches my eye, her thoughts seeming to collide with mine for a moment before she speaks again. She is my visual image, pictures of the possibilities of our imagined friendship spiraling through my head as I look at her.

MIA

Sense memory can evoke physical sensations and conditions. When we're offered a drink, we subconsciously recall taste to make a choice. We think of a place we love and we can see and smell it, even if just for a split second. This requires your imagination!

She invites us onto the stage and we collect in a circle. Realizing my eyes are still on her, I blush, remembering what she said in our first class, that our physical life speaks for itself. I try to relax, nervous about what my subconscious might tell people that I've not given it permission to tell. Around Mia, I feel like a ball of luminous energy. I can still picture Grace flirting on the opposite side of the courtyard—obvious just from how she was standing. Tell me I'm not that transparent. Mia pushes her sleeves up her elegant arms and asks for a sensory state.

ELLE

Cold.

MIA

Circle the stage as though it's cold.

We set off, briskly.

Remember a time when you were really cold. Imagine exactly how it felt and how you responded. Feel your toes starting to ache, your fingers turning numb, your knees shivering, your shoulders hunching.

I ball up my fists and cross my arms, tucking in my hands and my chin to stay warm. The wind is picking up, she says. People have turned up their collars and are bracing themselves against the imaginary chill.

After a few minutes, Mia relaxes, tells us it's summer. From the corner of my eye I see Ryan unbuttoning the collar of his shirt.

MIA

Close your eyes. Feel the heat of the sun on your face. Smell the summer air, the fresh-cut grass. Hear the birds singing, a lawn mower in the distance. Imagine that you're standing in bare feet, there's grass between your toes. Feel it—moist and cool.

I start to feel the grass beneath me.

Step from the grass onto a picnic blanket. It gives softly under your feet. You sit down.

She tells us now to lie down where we are and get comfortable. I settle on my back, closing my eyes again as people move about me.

MIA

That's right, Phy. Close your eyes, everyone.

She called me Phy. It sounded beautiful. I don't open my eyes but I imagine her looking at me. She waits for everyone to settle and when she speaks again her voice is soothing:

> You're lying on the blanket in the warm sun, your eyelids glowing, everything quiet except the birds singing. Just in your imagination, reach out and run your hands through the grass, catching it between your fingers. You pluck a buttercup and rub the soft petals between your fingertips. Sit up in your imagination and see the picnic spread beside you on the blanket. Take a strawberry from the tub and bite into it. The sweet juice runs down your chin, you wipe it away. Have a sip of the icy lemonade, tart and cold, the beads of water on the bottle cool and wet in your hand. Your eyes are getting heavy in the bright sun. Someone sits down on the blanket beside you . . .

She goes on and, guided by her voice, I'm carried away, beyond grass and sounds on a warm day. She's the one there on the blanket beside me, the reality of her voice colliding with the pictures playing in my head. When she tells us to open our eyes, I'm slow to let in the light. The stage seems blindingly bright and we sit up as though we've spent the duration of class somewhere else. I catch sight of you beside me—I didn't realize you were lying so close. We get to our feet. Mia's voice is quiet, almost a whisper. *See you next time*, she says.

She stands at the door when we leave class. Some days she says my name when I pass her. Every day I wait and see if I'm a simple good-bye, or if it's "Bye, Phyre." "Phyre" changes my day. We're reaching the door as she hushes us.

MIA

It's the theater trip next month. I'm running a scene-study class every Tuesday at lunch to read the play we're seeing. Come along if you're interested.

Interested? I drop my gaze to hide any visible sign of the excitement she's ignited dancing behind my eyes. They're still giving me away as I tuck in behind you and Kate at the door. Mia smiles at you, then at me, then at Eva behind me. *Bye*, she says. Just "bye."

.....

MY BEDROOM. THAT EVENING.

I close my door on the world and collapse onto my bed to stare at the ceiling. I stretch my arms out beside me, finding the button on the radio with a fingertip to fill the pressing silence so I can quell the ever-present rising hum of thoughts in my head. Music fills the room. Everything, it seems, is against me! I listen to the song that shouts back at me as if it can hear the thoughts pursuing me. *It started out as a feeling, which then grew into a hope, which then turned into a quiet word, and then that word grew louder and louder . . .*

MOM

Honey!

Mom, calling from downstairs. I press my hands to my temples to keep out the words that reel through my head anyway. I have a crush on a girl?

MOM

Supper!

I swing my legs to the floor, prize myself up off the bed, ignore the static tuft of sticking-up hair caused by dragging my head across the duvet, and head downstairs to stoke the embers of the fire that keeps me going.

. . . . . .

PEELE'S. AFTER SCHOOL.THE NEXT MONDAY.

Settled on a stool at the counter near the window, hands curled around a chai tea, I'm tired of feeling sorry for myself. We said good-bye earlier at the school gate but, tempted by the pleasant anonymity of *girl sits alone at coffee-shop table,* I came in here. Sitting behind my cup, amid passing shapes and the tinkling of spoons in saucers, I can dream about my romanticized future self: the free-to-be-me, respected, celebrated self, catching behind my sunglasses the stolen glances of people who recognize me from my illustrious film career. I see my reflection in the polished chrome of the coffeemaker: *girl with a milk-froth mustache watching the indifferent world go by,* and heroically concede the point to reality. A new influx of people moves past me in a blur, a hazy backdrop to my thoughts. There's a figure beside me, a wash of deep red, too close for me to see. Her voice:

MIA

Phyre. It's nice to see you.

Mia! Here! This is where I have to speak. To remember words. I'm trying to make the transition from thinking about her seconds ago to seeing her smiling before me. Still no words! It's like I've never said anything clever in my life.

ME

You're here.

Ah, blessed as always with the ability to make statements of genius at just the right moment. Did I expect her to evaporate out of context?

MIA

Yeah, I love this place.

She holds up her cup.

Have you tried their chai?

I overzealously pick up my own.

ME

Have I ever!

I do plenty of unnecessary laughing and more gesturing until:

MIA

Well, I should be going.

ME

Okeydoke.

Crap! I haven't said that since I was five.

She waves good-bye and leaves.

ME

(Head in hands)

. . . . . .

HOMEROOM. THE NEXT MORNING.

Sitting in front of you, I relive the embarrassment with agonizing clarity and redden at the memory. Chin resting on your forearms on the back of my chair, you look up at me with sympathy as we settle into a stupefied silence. Here's your chance to tell me it doesn't sound that bad . . .

. . .

. . . You take a ponderous breath.

YOU

She said no excessive gesturing onstage. She didn't say anything about real life.

I can't even bring myself to hit you.

ME

That's all you've got!?

The retelling didn't even do justice to the catastrophic nature of my performance. I find words for everyone else, sometimes they're even clever, but with her . . . I needed something that would leave her thinking of me, and she probably will. Because I'm a crazy person! Now the possibilities are flowing. *Sit down, have a drink. Tell me about your life, how you radiate something that makes me care so much.*

You're suppressing a smile. I glare at you, clearly not ready to laugh about it yet, and you bite your lip.

ME

She probably thinks I'm crazy, right?

Any more pearls of wisdom? Great. Thanks! No need to protest or anything: *Course not, Phy. I'm sure you seemed really clever . . .*

Your eyes have glazed over and now I'm not sure you're even listening. I puff out my breath and stare out the window.

. . . . .

CUT AWAY: THE SILENT SCHOOL GROUNDS, THE LAWN, A MOTIONLESS BLUE SKY.

FRONT GATE. SCHOOL. THE NEXT MORNING.

Sitting on the wall before first bell, I watch you walk toward me with a smile on your face, holding two cardboard cups, the early-morning sun behind you. We often meet at the gate to eke out the last moments of sleepy pleasure before school starts. We haven't spoken since yesterday morning; I went straight home after class. We don't have theater today so there's no need to concentrate and I haven't felt like talking since I excelled at looking like an idiot.

YOU

Morning. To cheer you up.

You hand me a cup that gives gently as I take it, sending a fount of frothy milk and the spicy sweet scent of chai through the drinking hole. I slurp it off the lid as you hop up on the wall beside me, setting down your book bag.

YOU

This is a do-over.

So you recognize that I'm still thinking about bombing under pressure!

YOU

Everyone gets tongue-tied. I'm sure it was more noticeable to you.

Nice try—it would have been noticeable to a newt. You lean toward me reassuringly:

I said "great" five times in a sentence once.

Then, taking a breath, you turn to me properly.

Clearly you really care about what she thinks, so we'll have a practice, for next time. I'll be Mia.

I laugh. You set down your drink and put on a cutesy face.

Hey, Phyre. Great name. It's nice to see you.

Still laughing, I take a swig of my chai, trying to play along.

ME

But you're you.

You hesitate, subdued, reverting to your regular voice.

YOU

What do you mean?

ME

I mean I'm not nervous around you.

YOU

Oh, right.

Relief flashes into your eyes for a moment.

Then use your *imagination*!

You fan out your fingers ethereally and I smile, even if you are making fun of Mia's class.

Evoke memories of Peele's. The sounds, the smells . . .

So when you give me my cue:

Have you tried their chai?

ME

Why yes, Mia. It is so creamy and delicious . . .

You nod your encouragement.

> ... like a flower's sweet nectar on a spring day. A golden pond caressed by the sun. Like, a cup ... of chai.

You can't suppress a laugh as I lapse into an impression of my inane jabbering from yesterday. And sitting here, watching you laughing in the sun, I know how lucky I am. You're still smiling as we slip off the wall and collect our things.

YOU

> Really, I think that went well. *I* found you fascinating!

ME

> That's me. Always something interesting to say.

I down the dregs of my drink as we head toward school. *Thanks,* I think, without saying it. I feel so much better. You're the best!

We're about to reach the steps when I hear the bell ring. *Shit!* I whip my head around and realize we're the only ones on the lawn. We're late! How did that happen? It feels like two minutes since we sat down. I grab your sleeve in a mild panic.

ME

No, I can't have a late! That means lunchtime detention. I *can't* have lunchtime detention.

Detention is Tuesday, the same day as Mia's scene-study class.

YOU

No need to panic.

ME

Too late!

After a second, my crafty-plan face takes over and I can tell by your raised eyebrow that you know what I'm thinking.

ME

Come on. We have to try!

And just like that, I'm running.

Seconds later, you're behind me.

YOU

Sure you want to do this, Phy?

ME

Sure as I've ever been.

I can hear your second eyebrow meet the first.

YOU
What's gotten into you?

Such a plethora of emotions in your tone, it's hard to make them all out. Confusion, amusement, resignation, possible admiration somewhere! And it's true. Something a little crazy has come over me. It's new territory. And so is the complex exploit of getting to homeroom unseen.

The principle is simple: the window in the corner of homeroom is behind a floor-to-ceiling bookcase, ground-floor access from the sports field. Make it to the window from the front of school, and you're home free. The trick: it's all about appearances. If you come out from behind the bookcase "with the right I've been here all the time" face, they get all turned around and are easily fooled.

I can see by your purposeful running that you've figured if we're going to do this, we're going to do it right, and as if on cue, you signal to my right.

YOU
We've got home ec in five, four, three . . .

The door opens and we flatten against the wall as Mrs. Kook appears from the main school building and crosses to the home ec block for first period. I smile a relieved *Thanks* and as we make the second run across the grass I start feeling the giddy tickle of a laugh. I've been known to laugh in tense situations. Uncontrollably. We have a fast enough pace that wind is whistling in my ears. The pure unexpectedness of suddenly having to run and a bloodstream full of sugar from my chai makes me feel airless. And yet, for some reason, this is the choice moment I pick to try to tell you why we're racing through school!

ME

There's something I've been meaning to say.

Now my laughing starts and, clutching my stomach, I think for a minute I might have to stop running.

I laugh when I'm nervous!

YOU

I already know that—

ME

No, that's not it!

Then there's the sound of footsteps from the blind spot beside the sports hall and I'm realizing that this is a poorly conceived plan as you reel to the left:

YOU

Plan B!

My forced whisper is louder than my speaking voice:

ME

This *is* plan B.

Plan A was "Be on time." I can tell from the way you're running that you're laughing. Hey, my laughing was panic induced! You're headed right for the footsteps and when I grasp your plan, I love you more than life. My look says "my hero," right before I leap the knee wall and drop down behind it into a ninja crouch. So it didn't feel so ninja-like. They always land with one knee bent, fingers splayed across the ground, and my knees are by my ears like a three-year-old squatting in a sandpit. I'm lucky I didn't split my jeans. The first voice I hear is Mrs. Keen, our English teacher. Even from behind the wall she's as annoying as she'd be if I were faced with her, because her expressions appear involuntarily in my head.

MRS. KEEN

Taking a turn around the garden, are we?

Despite there being no one to see, I make a face. I can't hear your reply but I'm pretty sure you say, *We are,* and I smile.

MRS. KEEN

Can I assume you have a good reason? You know I have to give you detention for being outside after the bell rings.

She makes it sound like a regrettable hardship but relishes every moment. Then, to my horror (and I use "horror" in its profoundest form) the door to the theater on my exposed side swings open and Mia steps out into the morning sun. I think I actually pretend to examine a buttercup. So now I'm the girl crouched behind the wall like I'm peeing in the woods on a field trip. Could this get any better? I squeeze my eyes tight shut for a second, hoping it might all go away, and when I open them, I'm still squatting over a buttercup with Mia still less than fifteen feet away. From here, it seems she's managing not to commit to a facial expression. I raise my chin, meet her eyes, and smile a desperate, desperate smile. This is all for you, I could say, but I just crouch here. I hear Mrs. Keen still talking, her voice sounding a mile away now despite the fact that she hasn't moved. Then, to my astonishment, Mia's gaze shifts right past me as if I'm not here at all and she crosses casually through the gap in the wall a few feet away to join Mrs. Keen. I hear feet retreating toward the main school building and, the next thing I know, your face appears over the wall. You stare at me where I am still squatting in disbelief.

YOU

This is no time for a pee.

ME

Ha!

—is all I manage and I remain a little stupefied as you take my hand and pull me up. I'm not sure what to make of Mia's help. I'm filled with a giddy mixture of horrifying humiliation and this delicious sense of complicity.

Moving again, we've passed most of the danger areas, so we head more slowly around the edge of school beside the playing fields and cut across the corner of the field hockey turf to the homeroom window.

ME

Detention?

YOU

Yep.

We're quiet for a minute. I take a breath, shaking my head at the great dearth of words.

ME

Thanks?

It comes out more like a question because clearly it's not nearly enough.

YOU

You're welcome?

Feeling a pang of vulnerability that you might now ask why it's so important that I stay out of detention, and because my reason will never make up for what you just did, I put all my attention into prizing open the unlocked window. As soon as I get my fingers into the gap and pull it wide, I brace my hands against the windowsill. The sill is only chest height but standing here it seems like a surprising challenge. You stoop to give me a leg up, and pressure-induced giggling threatens to return. I tip off balance, psyching myself into it. Then your hushed voice in my ear:

YOU

Someone's coming!

And I propel myself through the window, practically clearing the sides, like I was sitting on a rocket launcher. I make very little noise hitting the floor, all things considered, and when you don't appear for a second, I peer carefully through the window. You are doubled over. Laughing. It's my turn to raise eyebrows. And bare teeth.

YOU

Adrenaline. I knew it would be the fastest way to get you through the window.

ME

Very funny!

I'm considering closing and locking the window when I think of everything you're already done for me today, and I try a big-girl response: saying nothing.

When you've finally stopped laughing I help you through the window and only hit you once before perfecting my "There I was, reading" expression as we step casually around the door. The teacher on duty isn't even here yet, so I swallow my sweep of guilt as we join everyone else and try not to point out that you got detention for nothing.

. . . . .

THEATER. TUESDAY LUNCH. THE NEXT WEEK.

Today is Mia's first scene-study class—and your detention, which we haven't spent a lot of time discussing. The best I could do was a grateful hug as we went our separate ways, but my mind was already here. I push through the theater doors. There's Mia, alone, sitting in the front row. She has her hand on her forehead, hiding her face. She straightens up when she hears me, and smiles. It may be my imagination but she seems sad, her eyes glassy. Here's my chance, to be a cheering presence, a reason for her happiness. I head down the aisle toward her. Behind me, the doors swing open again and Kate appears, followed closely by Elle and Cara, then more people, everyone talking. Mia is up and cheerful, too enthusiastic, overcompensating, and the moment is lost.

We sit on stage in a circle as Mia talks about the play. She's doing her best, holding together, but when she's not talking, her animation falters, and she's lost in thought. She only comes back when she speaks again. Streamlined and studious, dressed in black today, she turns an apple over in her hands, apologizing that she didn't have lunch yet. She bites into it thoughtfully as she asks us what the objectives are for the characters in the play. Seeing her eat feels intimate, personal, and I forget to listen for a minute, watching the ripple of her jaw, the way her chewing pauses when she listens.

When the bell rings for the end of lunch, the rest of the class starts arriving, cutting short this newfound time with Mia. We're stacking the chairs away as I catch sight of you coming through the door. Mia has asked us to make a circle on stage and I signal for you to stand beside me.

ME

How was it?

YOU

Best fun ever.

ME

I knew it! I missed out.

You nod with a consolatory grin.

YOU

Next time!

Mia has stepped down from the stage to consult her planner so I whisk my head around to face you again.

ME

Have you noticed Mia seems down today? She isn't herself. Can you tell?

She's already on the steps, barely giving you time to shrug, and she dives in as soon as she joins the circle.

MIA

Emotion memory.

Hands go up.

BELLA

Evoking personal memories of similar situations to the one your character is in.

MIA

Exactly! Even if we haven't gone through the same thing, we can use something we've experienced to relate to the character. That way you can really explore what's true for you. Imagine how *you* would react.

She adjusts her collar. In some lights her black top is almost indigo.

Can someone give me an emotion?

EVA

Excitement!

MIA

Good. Excitement. Think about the most excited you've ever been. How did it feel?

Eyes to the floor, I focus on her voice.

MIA

Feel the butterflies in the pit of your stomach, the way they well up and make your throat feel like it will burst. You want to jump up and down, hug someone, pleasure pressing from your chest to the tips of your fingers.

I look across the circle to see if her own thoughts are playing across her face.

You'll each step forward, remembering that specific time, and react with the greatest intensity of excitement that you've ever felt. We'll go around the circle and every ten seconds the next person will also step in. The excitement should build until you've all stepped forward together. Then one by one you'll step out.

I try to conjure up the feeling I get when the lights go down at a movie or when the curtains open at the theater, when I want so much to be up there with the actors. And then there's the excitement I feel when I think about Mia.

MIA

Anyone like to be the first?

Sure! Ideally, but the idea of being that vulnerable is cementing my knees locked. Harmony puts up her hand. Presumably named even as a baby for her tiny aura, she makes no effort to challenge her reputation for being away with the fairies. She's not in touch with reality, everyone says. Perhaps her reality is just really pleasant.

She takes a step forward, freeing an easygoing burst of excitement. Ten seconds later, Elle steps in with energy flying in all directions. It's amazing how the vibe builds. I catch Ryan's eye, a few people to my right, and he's actually taking it seriously. Then, with my turn approaching, I let the heat of excitement well up in my chest, picture the bright lights, the vibration of music, the thunderous chorus of voices in my head. It all catches in my throat for a second and then I let it go.

We continue around the circle, getting louder and louder, until everyone's in, and the energy is electric. I steal a glance at you. Your excitement is more subdued than most but no less real. I'm surprisingly mesmerized by your face, lightened by this euphoric but silent intensity that flickers as we make eye contact. I want to know what you're remembering—I'll try to remember to ask. The sweep of people stepping out reaches me, the stage getting quieter, and as I step back I have a chance to look at Mia. She's more cheerful than she's been all day, the contagious excitement putting a genuine smile on her face. She waits for complete quiet before she laughs, gives us a pleased nod, and asks for another emotion.

ME

Sad.

She meets my eye. There are other suggestions ringing around the circle.

MIA

Relief! Good.

She rubs her hands together bracingly.

> Same thing. Remember a time when you've felt truly relieved—experience exactly how that felt.

Elle starts this time. I've felt relief, too many times to choose from. The time you fell out of the tree on your head and I thought I'd killed you: my heart pounding, panic in my throat, and then how I cried and laughed and squeezed and hit you when you sat up. I never wanted to care that much again and at the same time I wanted to hold on to the feeling forever. I relax abruptly as I realize it's already my turn to step out of the circle. Mia's gaze is concentrated on me when I look over. I smile with a mixture of emotions. She smiles back.

That keeps my spirits lifted for the remainder of class but as we're leaving, I hear Mia compliment Kate on being emotionally present. I try to tune out her words but they find their way in like a frequency that you can't stop yourself from hearing. I'm as present as I can be. How am I supposed to be more present than that? You've started talking now but I don't really hear, leaving my ability to concentrate behind in the room with Mia. I look deafly at your kind expression as we walk away, wishing that I could regain the contentment I used to feel when it was just you and me.

. . . . .

STUDY HALL. NEXT PERIOD.

It's the start of study hall. The day is catching up with me. I rest my chin on my forearms on the desk as the room moves around me. I squint to make patterns out of colors and light. Grace is perched in the middle of a circle of gossip girls like the needle of a compass. I catch Mia's name and lift my head.

ME

What's that about Mia?

The circle widens as we become an entire class of iron filings drawn into the magnetic field.

GRACE

I was just saying how Mia and her boyfriend broke up.

A rush of jealousy that someone else knows more about her than I do hurtles through my blood; then I think of her in class today and it makes sense.

ME

How do you know?

Grace relishes her moment of glory.

GRACE

Well, Jen told me that she sat at the table next to them at Sixpence last night. She said they were talking, and then Mia got upset and left during dinner. He stayed a few minutes and then he left too.

The *oohs* and *aahs* ring out, and then the magnetic field starts to lose strength. Grace continues.

She moved here especially for him. She'll probably leave now. I know I would. Can you imagine . . .

She keeps going. She has an active imagination but this sounds plausible. Even so, I want to throw something at her head to make her *stop speaking.* Mia's only been here a few weeks but already I can't imagine rooms and hallways without her. She's single?—

There's a flash. I blink and look left to see Ginny taking a photo. I put my hand in front of my face.

ME

Stop it!

GINNY

Relax! It's for the yearbook. Natural pictures are the best and how often are we all together?

ME

Every day.

I'm not excited to see how that one comes out. She does this all year. Find an awkward moment and trust Ginny to be there, snapping pictures to make it worse. Some people love getting in the yearbook. They dive into shots, wrapping their arms around people they barely know just to smirk at the camera.

Voices become murmurs, my thoughts spiraling. The study hall supervisor's chair is still empty. Maybe I could run for it before it's too late. The door opens and . . . *Mia*, of all people, comes in hugging a stack of files. She's everywhere! Grace sees her and starts whispering to Elle, prompting me for the second time to imagine throwing something at her head. I carefully examine the page of my book instead but the symbols have lost all meaning. I stare at my fingers flicking my pen lid open and closed. Despite my best efforts, she glows in my peripheral vision, like when you look directly at a lightbulb and then everywhere you look you see a spot.

▪ ▪ ▪ ▪ ▪

SCHOOL GATE. THE NEXT MORNING.

I'm standing at the gate, hands in my pockets, coat buttoned up. You're already inside but I'm hoping to catch a moment with Mia to console her about her breakup. I think I've missed her. How is that possible? I wait a few more seconds, kicking at the sea of red fallen leaves from the maples on either side of the gate. There's no satisfying crunch underfoot, they're damp and soggy. It's stupid to stay and wait but I can't leave just yet . . . My mind keeps changing the shapes and colors of approaching figures into Mia so that my heart jumps with expectation but when they get closer they're not even similar. I check the time. Great, now I'm late again! This is pointless. I turn, trying not to slip on the leaves—that would be the kicker—and glance over my shoulder one last time as I start toward the front steps.

. . . . . .

COURTYARD. SOON AFTER.

It's quiet and still. Class has started. School is so different without faces and voices at every turn: deserted, like you're in a dream and you know it's supposed to be school but it doesn't look the same. I think I see you at the English room window. The face disappears and I slip through the door into the hallway. I catch sight of the clock and pick up my pace, still imagining what I might have said: that she'll be okay, that she should stay? There are footsteps around the corner and somehow I know before I see her that it's Mia. In seconds, she stands before me—here in my head and then in these sudden unexpected places. I smile. She takes a second to register me and then glances up at the hall clock.

MIA

You're running late. Again? Better get to class.

I stand there, my mouth suspended between words and a strange sensation of wanting to cry. *Pull yourself together, Phyre.* She's a teacher, not your friend. Squashing the conspiratorial feeling from when she covered for me last week, I swallow, my cheek twitching with the effort of not crying, and start walking briskly toward class. I hear her footsteps walk the empty hall in the other direction, the silence embarrassing. My face burning, I flinch at letting myself imagine that waiting for her this morning could have been so different. The reminder of her authority follows me into class, late. Everyone stares.

▪ ▪ ▪ ▪ ▪

READING ROOM. LUNCH.

You've tried to catch up with me a couple of times today. You've asked what happened this morning but I don't want to talk about it. I'll probably never want to talk about it as long as I live. I didn't feel like eating lunch today so I came straight to the reading room, which is always quiet and empty, to curl up and die. It seems you know me too well. I can see you coming toward me through the square of glass in the door. I look back at my book and only hear the door swing open.

YOU

For a minute there I almost couldn't find you.

I look up from pretending to read and make a face at your sarcasm. You sit down beside me, more cheerful than I feel like being.

YOU

I'm glad I found you. There's something I've been meaning to give you for ages now. It's just never seemed like the right moment recently, with you being . . .

A bird in the tree outside catches my eye, landing on a branch that bounces under its weight. The shifting leaves intermittently expose the sun, blinding me every few seconds. You've stopped talking and are hunting in your bag.

The bough is still swinging, the sun in my eyes again, and again. The branch settles, a shadow across my face. The bird tilts its head, watching something, which reminds me of Mia, of the way she watches us in class. Now I'm really losing it—everything reminds me of her! I look back to see you frowning at me.

YOU

Phy? You're not listening.

ME

Sorry, I'm distracted. There's a lot going on, that's all.

I look at the book in my lap that I haven't really been reading and for some reason I can't shake the feeling that everything is terrible and I can't see how you're going to make it any better. The breeze shifts the leaves again, more fleeting sun.

ME

Anyway, I was kind of in the middle of something.

YOU

Oh. I just figured that if you were hiding you might need cheering up.

ME

Maybe I was hiding because I didn't want to be found.

Even as I say it I don't mean it how it sounds. And you're right. Mostly if I hide, it's to wait for someone to come and find me so I know that they care. I'm *glad* you're here. You stand up, taking me at my word, and shrug as you turn away.

YOU

Okay. See you later.

The door bangs sharply behind you and I sigh into the pages of my book.

▪ ▪ ▪ ▪ ▪ ▪

THEATER. MONDAY AFTERNOON. THE NEXT WEEK.

We haven't seen each other for a couple of days. We haven't even spoken since Friday and you didn't wait for me at the gate this morning, so I get the impression you've finally lost your patience with me. We agree there. Feeling depressed about Mia is one thing but not seeing you has made for a crappy weekend. Maybe I should just get over myself and tell you how I feel. I've been too embarrassed but I've *always* told you everything so maybe I can count on you, to help me see sense.

Mia's class is up next so I head into the theater hoping to find you. There you are—leaning forward to chat to Kate in the row in front of you. I head straight over, happy to see you, and settle myself down to wait for you to finish talking. When you finally pause, you look at me—as though I'm interrupting—in a way that I've never seen from you. It throws me. Plus, you're wearing yellow. Never in my life have I seen you wear yellow. I don't see you for a weekend and suddenly you're all sunshine. I hesitate, feeling uncomfortably like you're expecting me to earn this valuable moment of your time.

ME

Hi. Haven't seen you for a few days. Thought we could catch up.

Your expression is mixed.

ME

I've been meaning to talk to you, since . . .

Angry eyes. Still cross about the reading room. I get it but I persevere.

I could use your advice.

YOU

Yeah?

I swallow. You're not giving me the warmest sharing vibe.

ME

Well . . . it's complicated.

I look at Kate. She can sense she's in the middle of something here and semi-turns away, biting her lower lip. You smile at her, as if sharing some kind of joke.

YOU

Go ahead, Phy. Tell me your deepest secrets.

On a normal day I would smack you but this isn't playful. *I* came to make peace with *you,* so I rise above it and try not to tell you to *forget it* as that's not how I really feel.

ME

Can I talk to you or not?

You're considering it in an animated way, for Kate's benefit maybe, and I'm getting angry. With the *ultimate* worst timing ever, Tony appears beside me:

TONY

Hey Phyre!

He puts his hand on my shoulder. I notice he looks a bit more put together today and he's wearing a new pair of jeans. I try to smile.

ME

Hey!

Awkward pause.

TONY

I wanted to see if you wanted to go to a movie this weekend . . . maybe.

Shit.

ME

This weekend? I'm sorry, I can't this weekend but some other time for sure. Thanks though.

I give him a semi-thumbs-up, which then seems silly. I've never been very good at this. He nods, pauses as though he may say something else, and then walks away. You look at me, puzzled.

YOU

Some other time?

ME

Oh, you know I didn't really mean that.

YOU

Why did you say it then?

—!! Everyone else has arrived so there's no chance to ask *What the hell is with you?* I turn my attention to Mia, as usual. She is perched against the front of the stage and seems cheerful, not sad or distracted about her breakup like I thought she still might be. There go my hopes of being her shoulder to cry on, deflating with an audible whistle inside my head. She presses her fingertips together as she talks about her plan for the class.

MIA

Today is about listening.

I spare you a look of irony.

Really listening onstage is essential. We never know what's coming next. We're not exchanging lines, we're responding to a thought with a thought. Remember when you were a kid—didn't you think the aim of sword fighting was to clang your swords together? Really, you aim for the person and they deflect the strike. Acting is the same.

Everything you do is a response, not a preconceived pattern of one, two, one, two. Volunteers?

I have zero intention of volunteering today so I purposely look at the floor.

Phyre!

Yes. That *would* happen. She can tell I want to curl in a ball. I feel almost angry. When I catch her eye, I hope she can tell. To make matters worse, she calls *you* out as my scene partner. You slip off your jacket and we clamber equally reluctantly up on stage, standing side by side as if caught in headlights.

MIA

Contain your enthusiasm! Everyone's going to try this.

She smiles at me, igniting that spark in my chest. I try not to respond, setting my jaw, but despite my anger and despite feeling my heart sink every time I think of our last meeting in the hall, I smile back.

MIA

Can either of you fence?

My eyebrow shoots apprehensively skyward. I needn't shake my head, my expression has it covered.

MIA

Physical activity is a great way to stay in the moment. We'll try an exercise that combines fencing and karate.

Your cheek shifts into a smile that from this angle looks smug. Probably because you are—at the thought of my pinkness and sweating.

MIA

Think of this as a physical conversation.

I'll give you a physical conversation. I want to grab your sunshine-yellow shoulders and give you a shake.

MIA

The aim is to tap the shoulder or hip of the other person, their left side with your right hand, and vice versa. To defend yourself, swing your forearm on the same side up in front of your shoulder or down in front of your hip. Simple, right?

She smiles.

Keep it steady. Remember, you're communicating. Recognize that their action causes your reaction. Take it in turns, so the person who just blocked takes the next tap. Gentle. Go!

You reach out almost instantly for my left shoulder and I swing my forearm into your path. Pretty Karate Kid–esque if you ask me. I can't suppress a smile, and go for your left hip. Your forearm meets mine before I'm even close. We go on like this, your taps getting faster, but I'm equally committed. You swing for my right shoulder—there's sting in your effort. *Gentle!* She said *gentle*! You meet my eyes; you know me well enough to see you're pissing me off. It seems only to fuel the fire and, eyes locked, we're getting more determined. I started angry, this isn't helping. It's just getting more intense and I'm considering trying to concede with my eyes when:

MIA

All right! A nice example!

I relax, rubbing my forearm and knitting my brow at you.

The next step—the same idea with words.

She looks at you.

Let's imagine you're in homeroom. Phy, you're going to come in with a purpose. First—

She beckons me over. I take my time. I still want her to know that I'm angry. When I reach her, she cups her hand around my ear and puts her lips so close I can almost feel them. I hear her swallow.

MIA

Come in with something really important to say. Raise the stakes for yourself.

She straightens up and I return her nod somberly. She holds my gaze for a second and I try to make mine say everything that needs to be said. Then you step up and she whispers something to you. There's still a faint smile on your lips as you take your place onstage.

MIA

So, fill in the story for yourselves. Think about your objective, and watch how a second person's objective can act as an obstacle. When you're ready.

As I go behind the curtain I can hear you setting the stage. Then, after a minute of picturing myself in the homeroom hallway, I walk purposefully into the room and meet your eyes. Sitting on a chair in the middle of the room, you look up at me briefly, not long enough to give the impression you're happy to see me, and then turn back to your book!

ME

Hi. Sorry to come at you all out of the blue like this, but can we talk?

You glance up at me, and then settle your eyes back on the page in front of you.

YOU

I'd love to but I'll catch up with you later.

I pause. This is too familiar. Using reality against me! Not fair. I'd walk right back offstage if I could. I grit my teeth.

ME

It'll only take a minute, I promise . . .

I slide a chair over to the desk and you push away from it. Surprisingly hurtful. Remembering my purpose, I press on.

ME

Can you listen to me for a second?

YOU

We'll talk, I promise, but I can't right now.

ME

Even for a second? Please, just listen.

I see your eyes flare with something all too real.

YOU

You're asking *me* to listen?

I can see your retaliation pressing to escape, and then:

> You are so caught up in your own little world that you have no idea what's going on with the rest of us. Suddenly you want to talk to me, and I'm supposed to jump at the chance? Well, sorry, I can't be ready just because you are. I have my own things to deal with but what would you know!

The words ring painfully true; humiliation fills my chest. The line between this exercise and life is way too blurred. I stare at you. Faltering, I find anger much easier to experience, and hear my defensive words cut through the silence.

ME

Well, then I can't imagine why you would want to be friends with me in the first place!

My voice cracks, making me sound less resilient than I'd hoped. I swallow, and look at the floor.

Mia's voice pulls me from the moment. Not far enough.

MIA

Excellent. Very dynamic! Great commitment.

I look at her and for a second see her as puppet master, finding ways to humiliate me. But she has swept on and is cheerfully calling out the next pair. I shake my head free of stupid thoughts as we return to our seats. This is a side of you I've never seen before. You're finding courage onstage to speak your mind. You glance at me once but not again until the end of class.

. . . . . .

EMPTY THEATER. AFTER CLASS.

Everyone else has left. Without exchanging a word we have both stayed behind, a silent agreement that only years of friendship can achieve. As the door swings shut behind the last person, we're quiet for a minute.

YOU

What's going on, Phy?

I realize now that there isn't much I can say without sounding stupid. I'm looking at my shoes so I don't see you getting something from your bag.

YOU

Here, I've been meaning to give you this. I've been carrying it around since we were at the bookstore on the first day of school.

With a sinking heart, I see the filmmaking book I noticed you buy.

You seemed to like the class, so I thought you might like this. I've been waiting for the right moment to give it to you . . .

You set it down on the seat in front of me, shoulder your bag, and start walking up the aisle toward the door. Anger would be easier to take from you than this. I pick up the book and run after you.

ME

Wait. I do like it. I love it. I know I don't deserve it, but it's perfect. Thank you.

There are still the lines of a frown etched in your forehead. I haven't said the right thing yet.

ME

You're right. I've been really caught up in everything. I'm sorry.

We lock eyes. When you shift your gaze, I move to be in your eye line again. After a moment, I see the beginning of a smile in your eyes that hasn't even started toward your mouth but I know you.

ME

We'll be okay, right?

You turn to me as we head out of the theater. A familiar feeling is emerging between us again.

YOU

Ehh . . . Think I might pick a shiny new friend.

ME

Totally! I know I would. Nice T-shirt by the way. Yellow. Cheerful!

YOU

Yeah, thought I'd try something new.

ME

With that and a new friend, you'll be golden.

YOU

I'm excited.

I laugh, feeling the relief of having you back wash over me. For the first time in a few days I feel almost normal again—everything the way it should be. And I know that now is not the time to tell you anything. In this second, I like things just the way they are.

. . . . .

PEELE'S. THURSDAY. AFTER SCHOOL. A FEW WEEKS LATER.

The burnt-orange apron? Yes, mine! Peele's standard issue, which I wear with pride. The kind of pride you manufacture to hide embarrassment. The coffee cup: not mine but on its way to table 7 if I can remember which table is 7. It's only been a week since we were walking past and you pointed out the "Part-time help needed" sign in the window. I was running low on spending money, and with the theater trip and a few new movies I can't wait to see, the apron was a concession I needed to make.

We're back on track, you and me; at least I think so. It's taken a couple of weeks but with time and my efforts to act like a normal person, I think we're okay. We've never had a real fight before, so I hope so. I'm not sure I realized how uneasy it made me. I still feel relieved every time I see you smile at me each morning.

It's my first day so you've come in to surprise me, for moral support you say, settling into a window seat in the corner as the bell on the door dings. I don't look up, it dings every few minutes. The next moment, *guess who* is here, sitting down at the table next to yours! I knew there was a chance but I can't believe she's come in already! And she's alone; this is the perfect excuse. She's even more beautiful when she doesn't think anyone is looking. I start toward her table, reaching into my apron pocket for my pad. Another *ding*, and when I look up she's standing to hug the tall skinny girl who has just come through the door. Feeling my cheeks burn, I slip into the store cupboard and stare at the Sweet 'N Low for a second's reflection to pull myself together. When I reappear, smoothing down my apron self-consciously, you're gesturing helpfully to Mia from behind your menu in case I haven't noticed her. She's dressed more casually than in school—jeans and a silk scarf knotted loosely around her neck, with hoop earrings. It never occurred to me she would look so different on her own time. She's talking cheerfully to her friend now, an intimidatingly chic fashion type in a shirt with ruffles. Picking my moment, I swan toward them. My apron pocket catches on the corner of the counter and it stops me short, sending the croissant I'm carrying flying off its plate. Fortunately the sound of a falling croissant hitting the floor is a mere rustle, and I carry on as though the plate has always been empty and the croissant has always been on the floor.

MIA

Phyre? I didn't know you worked here.

ME

Oh, hi. I didn't, till today. It's just for the apron. I think the amber brings out my eyes.

She laughs. Hear that? I made her laugh. *A beautiful sound!* Draw attention to the apron, I thought. Preemptively agree I look stupid in case they think I haven't realized.

MIA

Suze, this is a student of mine.

Suze looks up at me and smiles, turning back to Mia almost immediately.

SUZE

Oh right! I can't get used to the fact that you're teaching already.

MIA

Crazy, I know!

I stand here like a lemon, thinking how much younger Mia seems in her own life, separate from us. They're smiling politely now, waiting for me to continue. I start, enthusiastically, then realize I'm being too cheerful—they might think I really like working in a coffee shop and have no life—so I bring it down a notch. I prop my hand against the redbrick wall beside them, which makes me feel like the guy who rests his arm on the back of your seat in a movie theater, so I remove it almost as fast, focusing on my pad. Small talk over, I forget to ask Ruffles if she wants a small or a large raspberry rooibos and, pretty sure I talked too loudly, stroll back to the counter with nothing on my pad but the doodle of a house. *Phyre! Crap.* I can't remember what Mia asked for. *Get it together!* I look at the corner of my pad, feathered into something like a flower, as if that will help. This is ridiculous. I'm too preoccupied with being engaging to perform the simplest task? I panic inwardly, poring over the menu to look for something that sparks my memory. Could be anything! Twirling my pen—I drop my pen, pick up the pen—I glide through the shop to you. You know me well enough to recognize a little panic. I pretend to engage you in polite conversation:

ME

(Quietly)

Help! I can't remember what Mia asked
for—it's gone right out of my head.

Puzzled, you peer at my pad and, seeing my useless origami, you bite your lip.

YOU

At least your pad looks nice.

ME

Thanks!

I glare. *Be helpful.*

Did you hear?

You gaze thoughtfully in recollection but I know that face! I know you heard and you're leading me on. You *hmm* uncertainly and I threaten you with a pinch. I have a killer pinch that you've learned to fear.

ME

Tell me . . .

YOU

All right, all right!

You grin and push away my hand.

Jasmine tea.

ME

That's it! I love you!

I give you a rushed hug.

You're the best.

When I straighten up, Mia is looking, and I laugh, embarrassed, saying something about friendly service, and flow busily but serenely back to my station.

. . . . .

CUT TO: LATER.

I'm frothing milk—still not something I'm good at; it deflates in front of my eyes by the time I reach people's tables—and Mia comes up to the counter as they're leaving. Seeing her approach, I turn off the milk frother to be casually available.

MIA

Thanks, bye.

ME

Oh, bye.

Heart fluttering, I twirl the sprig of mint sitting on a saucer I cleared earlier. She is still there:

MIA

Hey, I'm glad to see you so engaged in class. Can you meet me after school tomorrow? There's something I want to talk to you about, if you're interested.

Me. Interested! *Don't say okeydoke!*

ME

Sure!

MIA

And I'll see you on the theater trip tonight?

ME

You certainly will.

She begins to turn away, and I swallow. Here's my chance to find the courage to speak, to show her I'm thoughtful:

Mia?

The first time I've said her name to her face.

I heard that things didn't work out with your boyfriend and I'm sorry.

She turns back to me and smiles.

MIA

Thanks for saying so, but plenty of good has come of it. Right?

She means me? Probably not; why would she? But my heart skips three and a half beats before my body shouts at it in protest. I smile out loud.

She walks away and I resist the urge to dance. I was a veritable genius compared to last time. I absentmindedly nibble the corner of the mint leaf. Then I remember that it's someone else's and I spit it into the palm of my hand.

▪ ▪ ▪ ▪ ▪

THEATER TRIP. SCHOOL STEPS. 7 P.M.

I breathe in the fresh sweet air. Evening hours spent with Mia—Mia, who wants to speak to me tomorrow! If we were watching a shoe for two hours I would go if it meant being with her. It's a gorgeous crisp night. The temperature has dropped and everyone's shivering. Right now, I like shivering.

It makes me feel alive. Elle looks silly in a short skirt. She's squeezing her knees together to generate warmth. I've knotted my scarf and buttoned it in against my chest but I've forgotten my gloves so I fold my arms and tuck in my hands and chin. Ryan takes it as a hostile pose and calls across the grass:

RYAN

Blah-blah-blah-blah-blah.

Today, everything bounces off. Mia wants to meet with me and it is a secret joy that fills me with importance and expectation. Looking at people grouped on the steps I think with a pang of excitement that I have reason to feel special, and I imagine, with a new sense of entitlement, the evening ahead. I went to all Mia's lunchtime scene-study classes so I have some knowledge of the play we're going to even though my intention to dazzle her with bright remarks was compromised by the thoughts that take over when I'm in her presence.

When my mind returns to the steps, you're kindly holding out your gloves to me—but at that moment Mia comes down the path with Mrs. Keen and I forget about the cold. Everyone is flooding forward to the waiting bus. I hang back, reaching halfheartedly for your sleeve, aware of our proximity to Mia in the failing light. I'm hoping to sit up front with her, find out more about her. Chatting to Cara, you push ahead with her onto the bus and drop into a seat halfway back, reaching out to save space for me. You see me lingering and peer quizzically over the seat backs. With Mia in mid-conversation, I dismiss my tinge of disappointment—maybe we'll talk later—and make my way back to you. Given the rocky start to our friendship this year, it's probably a good thing.

. . . . .

THE BUS. SOON AFTER.

Quiet ride. I've been trying to be more open with you recently, so I should tell you my news about tomorrow. Tucking up my knees, I lean against you. You shift your weight, to accommodate me maybe—still, you feel strangely tense. I can't see your face because you're looking out the window but it's getting dark out so I catch your vague reflection in the glass. I'm about to speak when Cara's face appears over the seat in front.

CARA

Hey, kids. You're quiet!

Neither of us replies.

Pipe down. Don't make me come back there.

She wedges her face between the seats.

You're a wacky pair!

I smile and you do too.

How about this theater malarkey? Not bad. Phy, I've got a new video camera. Maybe we could play around with it over the weekend?

I smile and nod. Sounds like something that could get Mia's attention. We're nearly there and up at the front of the bus she's turned and is kneeling on her seat. She calls above the rising hubbub.

MIA

Collect a ticket from me as you go in, everyone. And pay attention tonight. You're going to have a paper to write.

People groan. She smiles.

. . . . .

THEATER FOYER. MOMENTS LATER.

We're crowding through the doors of the theater, past the review posters with stills of the cast and printed quotes: *Thrilling. A tour de force. Mesmerizing from start to finish.* Excitement pulses in my chest. This is what I want, to have my picture with a quote beneath it in a theater like this. We crowd past the bar to the mezzanine stairs, carpeted in plush crimson and studded with tiny bulbs. At the top, Mia stands beside the velvet curtains framing the doors to the auditorium. She hands out tickets as we pass her. I take mine and smile. She doesn't see me.

▪ ▪ ▪ ▪ ▪

THEATER AUDITORIUM. FIVE MINUTES LATER.

Mia takes her seat in front of me across the aisle as the giant chandelier dims. I look at her in the darkness, the curtain rising. She's looking at me! No, what I thought was the light in her eye is her earring glinting in the aisle lights. My eyes adjust to the dark and I can see the same concentrated expression she has in class when she watches us. The stage lights come up, finally taking my attention. I imagine myself up there with the lights, the audience, the adrenaline. It could be me, I know it could, and every moment I sit here, I wish more and more that it was.

▪ ▪ ▪ ▪ ▪

THEATER FOYER. INTERMISSION.

We crowd into the bar area at intermission and watch people swan away from the bar with their wineglasses, making comments that sound like the posters. We have just found an alcove when I see Elle with her arms around someone. I crane my neck with curiosity and swallow my reaction. She's kissing Tony! Tucked over by the bar stools, in a corner lit by a blue bar light that makes her yellow top look green, they're making out. So, the skirt did the trick! I elbow you in the side and point them out. You make a "to each their own" face. Turning away, I can't help thinking about Tony's lanky embrace—I guess the boat has sailed there, then. I hadn't heard anything about him liking Elle all of a sudden and that gets to me. It's not that the attention had been nice but it seems fickle. I'm more certain than ever that Tony is not what I want—maybe I'm just a little envious of how much simpler it would be. I flick through the program and we talk about the play instead. You're sweetly sincere, so I manage to forget about the goings-on in the corner and look forward to the second half. A brassy bell rings to send us back to our seats, and I scan the crowd for Mia as we herd back into the auditorium. She is talking to Kate, in the attentive way I've seen before. I look instead at the chandelier and push away my feeling of jealousy, a sensation I've come to hate more than any other. I wish I never had to feel it again.

▪ ▪ ▪ ▪ ▪

THEATER FOYER. AFTER THE PLAY.

We traipse out of the auditorium into the glare of the foyer. Seeing a play stops time—makes the real world seem so harsh. I blink in the light and, realizing that I managed not to think about anything else for the past hour, I cherish the moment. The sight of Mia disappearing through the doors into the night ahead brings back my excitement for tomorrow and the familiar brow-furrowing pang that seems always with me nowadays. We follow her out and, under the light of the evening street lamps, I remember the faint sense of importance that I started the evening with. She hasn't spoken to me yet. The evening wasn't what I thought it might be but there's always tomorrow. Tonight I'm happy to slide in beside you in the darkness of the bus.

You lean against the window, and I lean against you, and we watch the lights go by in silence.

▪ ▪ ▪ ▪ ▪

MY KITCHEN. FRIDAY MORNING.

Meet me tomorrow is now today. It feels like forever since yesterday and yet today came so fast. By the time I got home last night, my anticipation had tripled and I couldn't sleep. In my head I practiced appropriate responses to the possible conversations we could be going to have. I've spent an hour getting ready for school and this afternoon still feels like an eternity away. I'll go crazy! I've had a few spoonfuls of cornflakes and now I'm staring at the bowl, wondering why I would ever want to eat. Mom comes in and asks me if I liked the play. I'm too preoccupied to be chatty. *Not hungry?* she says. *Not like you, hon. Everything okay?* She hugs me as I leave for school and for a second I want to stay in that hug forever. Then, drawn by the thought of Mia, I am out the door.

▪ ▪ ▪ ▪ ▪

SCHOOL COURTYARD. NEARLY "AFTER SCHOOL."

Nearly there! Fifteen minutes to go; today, fifteen minutes feels like a lifetime. Final class of the day and we've been let out of history early. Given my concentration level, I couldn't even tell you it was history. I slip into the courtyard ahead of everyone, wondering where I should wait. I mentioned at lunch today that I'm meeting Mia, so you know not to stick around. The library! It's quiet—there's never anyone there—and, thinking that peace and quiet might help, I head quickly for the doors.

. . . . . .

SCHOOL LIBRARY. MOMENTS LATER.

There are bookcases on every side of me, as high as the ceiling. I head down an aisle. There's Harmony. At least there's the top of her head, her face in a book. She's one of the only two people in here. I stand in fiction and pretend to look busy. From the corner of my eye, I watch her expression as she reads. She seems so comfortable being who she is, so open that, forgetting I didn't want company, I go and sit down opposite her. She raises her eyes to me expectantly.

HARMONY

Hi.

ME

Hi.

Even her "Hi" is peacefully melodic. I speak before I'm even aware of the question forming in my head:

How come you don't try as hard as everyone else to be liked?

There is an impatient *shhh* from the *one* other person in here.

HARMONY

Liked?

I feel the sweaty panic of saying something stupid, and make effusive efforts to cover it up.

ME

I just mean you're different, different good. Great different. Yourself!

She smiles.

HARMONY

I'm kidding. I consider it a compliment.

I let my breath out.

ME

It *is* a compliment. I'd like to be more like you.

She smiles.

HARMONY

Really? Well, I can't see the point of being exactly like everyone else.

We share a minute of thoughtful silence. She looks at me carefully.

HARMONY

What are you so afraid of?

That's an excellent question! I'm still trying to find an answer when she continues:

Everything you're going through is perfectly normal.

My heart falters. I make sure my expression says "I have no idea what you're talking about," but I have a nervous inkling that I do.

HARMONY

I had the biggest crush on a friend of my sister once. She was amazing.

She goes on, completely unfazed.

It's funny how there can be something special about that one person, isn't it?

I'm that transparent!? The idea is mortifying but at the same time this girl has just given me license to feel something. Catching my stunned expression, she smiles warmly.

HARMONY

I've had a hundred crushes. There's a lot to be attracted to in this world. There's nothing wrong with that.

I swallow, staring at her and waiting for my heart rate to settle.

ME

I'm afraid of what everyone will say behind my back.

She puts her hand on the table between us in an unexpectedly comforting way.

HARMONY

Kind of ridiculous, isn't it. Since when should we be punished for a feeling like love?

Her startling wisdom imparted, she says she'll get back to her reading. Still reeling at her perceptiveness when the bell goes a moment later, I stand up impulsively, my purpose coming back to me with a jolt. This is the *now* I've been waiting for! Shouldering my bag, I struggle to find some parting word for Harmony. She returns my gaze, not seeming to expect me to say anything. So, with a simple nod, I make for the door and she waves her farewell. My rapid unchecked footsteps reverberate on the wood floor and the *shhh* from that one other person in here echoes after me.

■ ■ ■ ■ ■ ■

SCHOOL HALLWAY. SOON AFTER.

Mia is coming out of her classroom as I arrive, my heart already picking up pace with anticipation. She greets me with a warm smile.

MIA

Hi. Ready? Walk with me.

Ready? Yes! I swallow and fall in beside her. She is clutching a paperbound book. Heading through the doors with her, listening to her voice, I forget every second of expectation that has led up to this moment. We walk side by side across the grass toward the theater. She's talking about class, my vivid imagination. The seconds slow and to me we could be the only two people on earth. Turning onto the path, we sit down under the arch in front of the theater. I feel so awake—the texture of the bench under my palm, Mia's closeness, the crisp fall air. She says I'm a sensitive, honest actress and, dazed with compliments, I am missing the point.

MIA

So . . .

Finally! I was about to throw my arms around her neck and tell her that I love her too.

MIA

I'm putting on the fall play this year and I want you to audition.

Audition? Grasping the reality, I nod my head. Of course I was going to audition, I want to be an actress. But to know she wants me there. This could be perfect.

ME

Sure.

She claps her hands together, genuinely excited.

MIA

Excellent. Here's the script. Have a look at Lily.

She hands it to me, and I clutch it like a present. Kate appears at the end of the path.

KATE

Mia, you wanted to see me.

She says her name to her face like it's butter on her tongue. Mia is already up and walking away. She smiles back at me.

MIA

See you Monday for auditions, Phyre.

I sit beneath the arch as I process everything that just happened. So I'm not the *only* one who Mia has arranged to meet. That's okay. Maybe I blew it a little out of proportion. Even alone, I feel my face flush pink and my chest constrict with private embarrassment. As I find my feet and walk toward the gate, new (sane) thoughts start to take shape. At least this is my chance to spend time with Mia. My new sense of purpose intensifies as I walk; I'm recognizing with every step how imperative it is that I get this part. If I don't, I can't begin to imagine the jealousy that I'll have to live with—about all the time she'll be spending with someone who isn't me.

. . . . .

MY BEDROOM. THAT EVENING.

First thing when I get home from a tediously long shift at Peele's, I run upstairs and fling myself down on my bed, pulling Mia's script carefully out of my bag. Lying on my front, I tuck my hair behind my ears and press open the paper cover. Holly pushes through the door and jumps up onto the bed, stepping across the small of my back to find a choice spot on the windowsill. I reach to rub the top of her head, and then start to read . . .

. . . . .

THE PRICE HOUSE. EVENING. 1950.

The bedroom of Lily Price. A record player plays jazz. Lily, seventeen, a pretty, vivacious small-town girl, turns it up. She sweeps her hair out of her face and dances to the music. She puts on lipstick, curls her eyelashes, and then fastens her necklace and smooths it down beneath the collar of her satin dress. Abuzz with nerves and excitement, she is almost ready for her first date with Michael. She has dreamed of this moment. He should be here any minute.

The front doorbell rings. She takes one last look in the mirror, sprays herself with perfume, and runs down the stairs into the kitchen. Bobby, their farmhand, is sitting down for soup at the kitchen table. He grins at her affectionately.

BOBBY

Where are you going, Miss Price?

LILY

Never you mind.

BOBBY

But I do.

LILY

I'm going on a real date, Bobby, with a real man.

BOBBY

Fine by me. You'll come back when you know what's right for you.

LILY

You just see if I do.

She snaps her purse shut, shoots him one last glare, and stalks out the door as sexily as she knows how.

▪ ▪ ▪ ▪ ▪

MOM

Phyre.

I flip the play shut. Mom is calling from downstairs. I consider pretending I didn't hear but she calls again.

ME

Yeah!

I can't hear her reply, so I reluctantly slide off the bed and go into the hall. At the bottom of the stairs, I see *you* beside her, looking up at me.

ME

Hi!

Right now I'd rather read the play than anything but as I look down at your open expression and Mom disappears back into the kitchen, I figure I can spare a minute. Trotting down the stairs, I jump the last step and meet your gaze.

YOU

So what did she say?

You haven't taken off your coat yet so, instead of inviting you in, I pull my sweater off the peg by the door and we go into the garden. There's a chill in the air but it smells good out and we wander over to the tree house we built in fifth grade. "Tree house" equals plank between two branches, barely five feet off the ground, but it seemed death defying at the time. We squeeze side by side onto the plank, legs dangling.

YOU

So?

ME

Mia thinks I should audition for the play this year.

I look at you in the light from the windows of the house, wondering if your expression will give away the "Is that all?" that I tried not to feel.

YOU

Of course you should!

I smile.

ME

She gave me a copy and I had just started reading—

YOU

Oh, sorry, would you rather get back to it?

ME

No. No, that's okay.

Sitting in the tree beside you, staring up at the night sky, it really does seem okay. The breeze picks up and makes me shiver.

YOU

Cold?

I shake my head, even though I am a little. Then, forgetting that I wanted to be by myself tonight, I suggest we get hot chocolate and go up to my room to read the play together. We attempt a dismount at the same time, getting temporarily wedged together in the crook of the tree. After choreographing the maneuver, we head inside, laughing.

. . . . .

MY BEDROOM. SOON AFTER.

You're lying beside me with the play, catching up on the first scene. I roll onto my back and stare up at the ceiling, picturing Lily, excited and nervous. I'm caught up in imagining how I would feel when you reach your arm across my chest—to rub Holly behind her ear. I had completely forgotten she was there, still curled in a ball on the cushion on the windowsill! Not seeing my surprise, you keep your arm across me for another moment, rubbing her tummy. I watch her unfurl under your hand. Turning your attention back to the play, you ask me if I'm ready to read the next scene together. I sit up. The idea now seems somehow embarrassing. It feels more intimidating one on one than it would in front of an entire audience. Audition jitters maybe.

ME

You'll read Bobby?

YOU

I'll *rock* Bobby.

You encouragingly tilt the page toward me as you start reading the next stage direction.

. . . . . .

THE PRICE HOUSE. MORNING.

Whistling, Lily skips downstairs into the kitchen, buttoning her dressing gown. Exhilarated, she happily sets about making breakfast. Bobby's head appears around the kitchen door:

BOBBY

How's lover boy?

LILY

Bobby!

She tightens her robe across her chest, self-conscious.

For your information, I had a great time. He was a gentleman—it was a magical evening.

Her mind drifts back to her night, hearing the music, a smile spreading across her face.

And we're going out again on Friday.

Bobby's face falls. He tries to hide his disappointment, and says nothing for a second.

BOBBY

Right. Well. Got to get to work.

Lily looks after him as he closes the door behind him. She is surprised to see him leave, cutting their habitual banter short. The kitchen seems quiet now without him.

. . . . .

I snap the play shut.

ME

We don't need to do this now. I have the whole weekend to prepare.

YOU

Well, now I want to know what happens.

ME

Are you going to audition?

YOU

I was that good?

Silly question, you're not really one for the limelight.

ME

How about set design?

YOU

Or lighting!

You swivel my bedside lamp so it shines in my eyes and I squint, dazzled by the bulb, but still giving you my best red-carpet face.

ME

Definitely lighting!

Laughing, I push the lamp away, startling Holly, who jumps up and darts out the door.

ME

Think I'll make a good actress?

YOU

The best!

I smile. We sit in silence for a few minutes and I tip my cup to let the dregs of my hot chocolate slide down the side. These are the best evenings. I catch sight of the play and feel a pang of excitement. The clock on the landing strikes nine as I'm caught up in a renewed desire to make sure I get this part.

ME

Then there's work to do.

YOU

I can take a hint!

You roll off the bed and pick up your sweater.

ME

Night, then.

You stop at the door and smile—

YOU

Night, Lily.

. . . . .

SCHOOL THEATER DRESSING ROOM. MONDAY AFTERNOON.

Auditions today, and there are a lot of people here! Crammed into the dressing room backstage, I'm more nervous than I expected, sitting on a makeup table, pulse racing. I've been onstage before. I can do this. There's nervous expectation in the air—maybe it's all mine. Mia comes in and everyone falls quiet.

MIA

Thanks, everyone, for coming. Just give it your best and commit to the moment.

She says that like it's her mantra, and then pins up the sheet of paper she's holding. She glances in my direction as she reaches the door. I meet her eyes and know I'm up first.

MIA

The first pair when you're ready.

Less time to get nervous I rationalize as I stand up. Everyone's vying for a look at the list. She's paired me with Zach, a senior. I recognize him from the play last year. I smile in his direction as we head together into the theater.

. . . . . .

THEATER. MOMENTS LATER.

Standing onstage next to Zach, I look out at the theater, empty except for Mia in the third row. She asks for the first scene. I head upstage, evoking every emotion I've ever felt for a guy, coupled with this strange need I have to please Mia. The theater falls quiet . . .

. . . I hear the jazz on the record player, twirl a strand of hair around my finger and smooth it behind my ear. I run my finger over my lower lip, tilting my head to look at my reflection in the mirror. Nerves and excitement pulse through me, sending jitters to the tips of my toes as I smooth my hands down over my skirt. It's here—the night I have always dreamed of, imagined every time I've closed my eyes. It's really going to happen. I'm making finishing touches to my hair and—the bell—he's really here. Am I ready? Taking a last look at my dress, pleased with how it shapes my figure, I dance down the steps to the kitchen and Bobby—trust Bobby to be here! He stares up at me but, realizing that he's seeing me at my best, I don't mind so much. He asks where I'm going and, as I cross to the door, I hide my smile, liking that he wants to know and thinking that maybe I want to tell him. Because tonight I'm going to be the belle of the ball and everyone will be looking . . .

MIA

Thank you.

Mia smiles. And that's it!

We step down offstage as Kate pushes through the backstage curtain. Paired with Gabe, another senior, she doesn't even seem nervous. Behind the curtain, I let Zach go on ahead and take my time returning to the dressing room. I turn back in the wings and stand quietly for a moment in the dark. I can't see but I can hear Mia's voice and then Kate.

She sounds so real onstage, like herself. She's good—I'm newly intimidated. Before the scene ends I slip quietly away and for the first time entertain the real possibility that it won't be me spending time with Mia.

. . . . . .

SCHOOL HALLWAY. THE NEXT DAY.

We're being funneled down the hall with everyone else. Mia said she would post the cast list at lunch. Seeing a cluster of students at the notice board ahead, we speed up and join the cluster like sheep. The list must finally be there. It's all I've thought about. We're on tiptoes at the edge of the pack.

ME

Can you see?

YOU

Not yet.

We shuffle to the front as people peel off to the sides. I can see the top of the board:

CAST LIST

Everyone is still chattering as they mingle into the crowd. Then there is space and when people stop jostling me, I can see names. At the top, it says "Lily." And beside Lily: Me. Elated, I can't stop smiling. You put your arm around my shoulders and squeeze me to you.

YOU

Congratulations, hotshot.

Yes. I'm a hotshot.

. . . . .

PEELE'S. AFTER SCHOOL.

You said we should celebrate, so here we are! If Peele's isn't a celebration, I don't know what is. I floated here on a cloud and you've sweetly kept up with my excitement for the last half hour. I swirl my spoon around in the cup again, and giddily set it back in the saucer.

ME

Can you believe it?

YOU

Yep.

ME

Can you? I can't. I can't believe it.

I knew I *could* get the part, I'm just so relieved it's happened. I take a sip of my tea.

YOU

Jasmine tea. Never seen you get that before.

ME

No?

Today, I'm not sure I even care if you remember when we last came across it. You eye me carefully.

YOU

Nice?

ME

Delish.

YOU

Really?

ME

Yep.

YOU

You don't like it, do you?

ME

Nope. Tastes like a flower bed.

You laugh, shaking your head despairingly.

YOU

Not your cup of tea.

I roll my eyes and give you a token ha-ha before laughing genuinely into my muffin, loving life, but not jasmine tea, and remembering my reason to be happy.

. . . . .

MY BEDROOM. THAT NIGHT.

Hands behind my head, I lie contentedly in bed. It's better to be me right now than it ever has been before. I can't bring myself to close my eyes, to shut out the rosy hue that my new world has. Light shines through the gap in the curtains so I can still see the shape of the play on the bedside table beside me. My new sense of purpose is keeping me awake. I've been given time with Mia, glorious time that will be mine and hers, mine to be visible to her, earn her respect. When I let my eyes close, I can picture the lights and the stage, and the curtain call at the end of it all. I feel the rush, her eyes on me as I earn her approval. Maybe this is how I'll find a way to be happy being me.

. . . . .

THEATER. FIRST DAY OF REHEARSAL. AFTER SCHOOL.

I'm the first to arrive in the theater and I stare up at the lights feeling today like this is my place. This is where I'll prove myself. The rest of the cast is gradually assembling and I look around at the faces with a sense of belonging. *Come in character*, Mia said. I smile at Kate. She's playing Penny. Penny doesn't smile back. Gabe sits next to me; he's been cast as Bobby. I spare him a second glance. He looks strong and boyish, not like a theater type. I've seen him around and figured he was all about sports—the kind of guy who calls you "babe." He catches me looking and I feel the blood rush to my cheeks. He smiles and, close up, I see softness in his eyes. It's surprisingly disarming. His eyes stay on me but I'm not sure if he's looking at me or Lily so my blush is genuine. Zach strolls in at the last minute and sits by Kate. He's playing Michael, Lily's perfect date. He gives me a friendly nod as Mia takes her usual perch on the front of the stage.

MIA

So! We'll start at the beginning. The beginning for your character isn't the first scene, or the moment before the first scene. It's every moment in their lives up until the first scene. Know your character's history. Something I love to do is write a journal in character. Try to think like they do so you can fully inhabit their responses.

We start by introducing ourselves in character. I feel self-conscious but then Lily is too, so I embrace it. Mia calls us up to start the rehearsal. *Purpose*, I think as I get up onstage. I am Lily. I'm seventeen. I want to fit in.

Scene one goes smoothly enough, as I know it by heart. Gabe feels really real and present onstage, which makes him easy to respond to. I get caught up for a second in scene two, remembering our read-through in my bedroom. You put your name in for doing lights, so I know you're somewhere up at the control board, sitting in on the first rehearsal to get a feel for the play.

For the third scene, Sarah, a senior, steps up onstage. She's playing my mother and has embraced the role wholeheartedly. She's been in character from the moment she arrived today and even now takes her place as if it really is her house. Lily is ready for her second date with Michael:

. . . . .

THE PRICE HOUSE. FRIDAY NIGHT.

Lily stands on tiptoes at the kitchen window and watches for headlights in the driveway. She wears her best dress tonight—Michael is taking her somewhere special. He's not here yet, he must have been held up. Her mom finishes setting the table.

MOM

Remember, honey. Don't stay out too late.

LILY

Mom, I'm seventeen. Everyone stays out late.

MOM

All right. But that doesn't mean you have to.

Lily glances at the clock again. It's after seven. He should be here by now. Her dancing shoes are already hurting her feet.

Spotlight on the kitchen wall clock. The hands roll forward. An hour passes.

Lily, still in her dress, sits on the kitchen step, sobbing. She lifts her hands to wipe her eyes but she is wearing her new gloves—she doesn't want to spoil them. She pulls them off and wipes the back of her hand across her cheek like a child. Her mother comes over and sits down beside her, putting an arm around her shoulders.

MOM

I'm sure he just got held up, that's all. There'll be other nights.

LILY

(Between sobs)

No, there won't, Mom, I know it's not that. I'm not good enough for him! He's decided that it won't do to be seen about with me. He wants one of those rich girls. Everyone says so!

MOM

Oh, that can't be true, he'd be lucky to have someone as special as you.

LILY

It is true. He was just biding his time with me till someone better came along. Bet you anything he's out with someone else right now.

Lily takes off her jewelry.

They spend all their time at some girl's pool house. They're always talking about it. And they never invite me.

MOM

Well, how about I make you something to eat and we'll just wait and see if he stops by to make his apologies.

LILY

He's not coming, and I'm not hungry.

Lily stands up and kicks off her shoes.

I wish I'd been born someone else—

She takes the stairs to her room two at a time and flops face-first onto her bed, covering her head with the pillow.

▪ ▪ ▪ ▪ ▪

Energized, the first rehearsal at an end, I watch everyone flocking out of the theater and stay behind with Mia. My intention: to sound casual.

ME

Mia—

I'm almost touching her shoulder as she turns.

—Thanks so much for giving me the part.

She smiles.

MIA

You deserved it.

ME

Really?

She nods warmly.

MIA

When I look at you onstage, I see someone trying to deal bravely with emotions. That can be a lot more sympathetic than watching a person indulge them.

She picks up her file and we start together toward the doors. I'm glowing with the compliment.

You've seen movies where if you have to watch a minute more of a girl sobbing

you're gonna throw your popcorn at
the screen, right?

I laugh. She breaks into an impression of indulgent crying, shaking with sobs. I chime in and she chokes through her pretend tears:

MIA

I'm so sad. And I'm such a good actor.

My crying becomes laughing and so does hers. She shakes her head.

Give me trying *not* to cry and a quivering lip any day.

ME

Not too quivery!

MIA

God no! Never *too* quivery. Then you've almost got pretty-girl crying. And that's worse.

ME

Way worse!

We start pretty-girl-crying impressions, passing a few staring eighth graders in the hall.

Must not make a wrinkle.

MIA

Must not look ugly.

This ends in a similar way and it may be the best feeling I've ever had. She sighs.

If you're going to cry, there's an "I can't help it, creased-up face" happy medium.

She's still pretty, whatever her expression.

Ultimately, it just needs to be real.

We've reached the staff room. I feel like I've walked her home after a date. She turns squarely to me.

MIA

Never get overdramatic on me, Phy, and we'll be fine.

I quiver my lip and don't blink in the hope of achieving glassy eyes. She laughs again, heartily. I start walking away before she pushes open the door, not to outstay the moment—so that when I turn and wave over my shoulder, she's still looking.

▪ ▪ ▪ ▪ ▪

SCHOOL LAWN. LUNCH.

There's a warm spell and I'm sitting on the lawn, carefully situated where I know Mia walks by on her way to her seventh-grade class after lunch. With the glimmer of a new friendship, I'm even more excited to see her than usual. I have one knee curled up and the other stretched out, running my toes through the grass. Open on my knee is my copy of the play. No coincidence. I've planned, in the cool glow of early afternoon sun, for Mia to come along and see my thoughtful dedication. The *coolness* of the sun has taken me by surprise. Part of my plan was the emerald halter top I'm wearing but the day is not as warm as it looked. Sitting still for half an hour can make even a warm day feel cold and this sun is misleading. My bare shoulders still have their summer tan but goose bumps ruin the effect. I tuck up my knee, trying to look warm and relaxed, and focus on the play. So far, I've read the same paragraph eight times and I still don't know what it says. I can hear the words in my head but they have no meaning. My peripheral vision is working far too hard to allow for concentration. I am making an arc in the grass with my foot, and pluck a buttercup between my toes when I see Mia at the start of the path. I return self-consciously to the script and only look up again when I think she will be nearer. She has cut across the far side of the lawn and smiles when she sees me looking. She waves and keeps on walking. I paste on a smile. She is too far away to see that it's a glassy attempt to hide mortification. Maybe I looked too studious to be disturbed. I stare at the same paragraph, now not only cold but also without the will to warm up. When I find the energy to move, I pick up my bag and start back toward school to get ready for class.

. . . . . .

HALLWAY. SOON AFTER.

You're heading toward me with a smile.

YOU

Hey. You look cold.

ME

That's because I am.

YOU

Where were you?

ME

Reading.

You peer at me quizzically as if you'd like to know more but can tell you shouldn't ask.

YOU

Mia was looking for you.

I stop in my tracks.

ME

What? But I just saw her. *Kind of.* She didn't say anything.

YOU

Oh. She ended up talking to Kate, I think. Don't worry, it was just about needing someone to post the rehearsal schedule or something.

I almost laugh, overcome with the urge to slam something against a locker.

ME

That's just great! I'm waiting for her and she was looking for me.

YOU

You were waiting for her? I'm confused.

ME

At what point in the twisty-turny plot did I lose you?!

My exasperation escaped too fast. Here I am taking it out on you again. We're paused in the hallway on that knife-edge: where everything is aggravating me but I should just let it go. I rest my forehead on your shoulder with a groan.

ME

Sorry. Never mind. I was just hoping to see her, that's all.

You seem to be trying to understand but your forehead is still creased. We start toward class and I seize a fleeting moment of resolve.

ME

I don't know if I want to *be* her or *kiss* her but I know my heart is ready to explode.

We're still walking. Everything looks the same. We're both still here. The world didn't go up in a puff of smoke. I can't bring myself to look at you for a second but when I turn—

YOU

Bang!

I grab your arm, pressed warmly against mine, and laugh and laugh.

. . . . .

HOMEROOM. THE NEXT WEEK.

People are taking their seats as I come into homeroom and cross to my chair. There on my desk is something waiting for me! Not even taking the time to wave in your direction, I tuck my chair in behind me and pick up what looks like a book. I run my fingertips over the textured cover, examining the clasp keeping the pages together. It says nothing on the front so I release the clasp and open it to the first page. There, in calligraphy, in the top corner: *Lily Price. 1950.* It really is for me! I look more closely. It's like something from the fifties, the creamy pages blank, but each edged with a curly pattern. I look up, a smile spread across my face, and you're smiling back. We have a minute before first bell and I hold it up, beckoning you over. You look excited as you come toward me and I haven't even shown it to you yet! I present it, gleeful.

ME

I think it must be from Mia. It was right here on my desk!

Everything's falling into place.

Remember, she said we should write a journal in character. Its perfect, isn't it? Look how beautiful!

Struck by her kindness, I'm filled with a feeling of closeness to her. I hold it up to let you see. You look blankly over the cover.

YOU

No . . . Yeah, it's great. I mean, I hope it's helpful.

I nod my head, holding the book to my chest, overcome with pleasure at this moment in my life and happy that you're here with me.

ME

This play is the best thing that's ever happened to me.

You nod.

YOU

I'm glad you like it so much.

I'm already formulating in my head the first words that Lily would have put down on paper in 1950 as you return to your desk.

. . . . .

THEATER. AFTER SCHOOL. THE NEXT DAY.

At the end of rehearsal, I snatch up the first chance I've had to thank Mia for the journal. There was no time to mention it at the beginning with everyone here, so I coolly approach, with more familiarity than I usually have the courage for.

ME

Hey.

Holding the journal, I press my hand to its cover.

I've been writing as Lily in my journal, and I can't tell you how helpful it's been.

MIA

Oh, that's a great idea! I try to encourage it. I'm so glad it's something that you thought would work for you. And I'm always pleased to see initiative. Let me know how it goes.

I assure her I will and, replaying her words, tuck the book back into my bag as I walk out of the room. *Great idea.* I swallow, with a sinking feeling in the pit of my stomach. *Great idea.* She was full of warmth, sincerity, and not the slightest twinkle of recognition. Pushing thoughts from my head, I check the time and, turning down the hall, go straight to where I know you will be.

. . . . .

SCHOOL GYM. MINUTES LATER.

Basketball seems to have just finished as I get to the gym. I haven't even reached the doors when you and Cara push through toward me. I smile quickly at Cara, then take hold of your wrist and pull you to the side so we're not swallowed in a stream of traffic.

ME

Mia didn't give me the journal.

YOU

I know.

Just hearing the way you say it makes me feel sick. The framework that holds me together turns to jelly as I take a swing at your arm, and my voice comes out as a whine I don't recognize.

ME

Why didn't you tell me it was from you?

YOU

Because you seemed so much happier when you thought it was from her.

I fall a little farther. The matter-of-fact way you say it only makes it worse.

ME

No! I would have loved it just as much if I'd thought it was from you.

My voice comes out in a fraught tangle as I try to believe that's the truth. You're taken aback by the strength of my emotion.

YOU

Okay, okay, I know. You still would have liked it. It's all right.

I take a breath and try to pull it together.

ME

I wish you'd said something.

YOU

I didn't want to make you feel . . .

ME

. . . *Stupid!*

I almost lose it again. When someone tries to save you from your own stupidity it only proves that they think you are. Letting the rest of my air escape, I put my face in my hands. Slowly, I feel your arm around me, which makes no sense. How can you be so forgiving when I make these kinds of mistakes?

ME

Sorry, I just feel like an idiot.

Reluctantly, I think back. There was nothing to suggest that it was from Mia. Nothing at all. That's just what I let myself believe, for no reason. And I was so convinced! With a deeper pang of embarrassment I remember how you came toward me, probably because you expected the thanks that you deserved. You squeeze my shoulder gently.

YOU

Hey, Phy. Not everyone is staring yet.
You wanna try and bag the last two?

I almost smile as you gesture toward the *only* faces not looking this way. We turn toward the courtyard and, with my eyes still on the ground, I let out my best strangled wail.

ME

Did I get 'em?

YOU

You got 'em!

Side by side, we start walking, and despite your efforts my thoughts return to the journal.

ME

I love it anyway—

I repeat it twice more, and you nod as convincingly as you can as we head to the gate.

. . . . .

HALLWAY. MORNING BREAK. THE NEXT WEEK.

I'm ambling slowly to class, past the theater notice board. There's a voice behind me. I spin around to see Tony coming toward me. I haven't seen him with Elle recently—I think their love lasted all of two weeks! The customary:

TONY

Hey!

ME

Hey!

TONY

So, I hear you're doing the play.

ME

Yep.

TONY

I was going to try out but it clashed with football.

Ryan, barreling down the hallway toward us, interrupts the moment as always.

RYAN

Hey, Tony. You're persistent!

Tony blushes and Ryan thumps him on the back.

Sorry, man. Didn't mean to embarrass you.

The conversation fizzles out and Ryan throws his arm around Tony's neck in a semi-headlock as they turn away.

RYAN

Forget it, man. She's cold.

Tony shrugs him off as you appear. For a vivid second, I imagine punching Ryan in the face (Tweety Birds circling). Or I could fling my arms around Tony's neck and kiss him like everyone else—to protect myself from comments like that. I choose neither. And in my hesitation you find your protective streak.

YOU

Don't talk about her like that!

Ryan stops. I can see him toying with the idea of sarcasm, or something really eloquent like "shut up."

RYAN

Come on, I'm just playing.

YOU

Yeah, you're funny. Go play with someone else.

Ryan scoffs but I can tell it's because you got to him. Tony turns back, trying to regain the tone he started with.

TONY

Well, good luck in the play.

It doesn't work. He leaves with a smile but it's half-assed and I wonder if this time he really will give up. The hallway is quiet again.

YOU

You okay?

ME

(Lying)

Fine!

. . . . . .

THEATER. AFTER SCHOOL. THE NEXT DAY.

Everyone is in the theater. Sarah, in character as usual, gives me a kiss on the top of the head on her way past. I look to see if Mia is here yet, as if that were necessary. I can see her without looking because of the place in my consciousness that is reserved just for her. She pushes through the door, her mind sweetly engaged by something far away, but she smiles when she sees me looking. I watch her set down her bag as I climb up onstage behind Sarah. Is Lily's life any simpler than mine? Maybe hers will put mine into perspective. My moments of perspective seem only to last until the next time I see Mia.

. . . . . .

THE PRICE HOUSE. SATURDAY EVENING.

Lily's mother stands at the sink, humming. Outside, Bobby arrives nervously at the front door in a suit and tie, with his hair neatly combed and a bunch of flowers in his hands. He rings the doorbell. As Mom crosses to open it, she sees him from the window brushing his shoes against the bristles of the hedgehog boot cleaner. She opens the door:

MOM

Well now, don't you look handsome. And such clean shoes!

BOBBY

Thanks, Mrs. Price. I heard that Miss Price didn't have the best of evenings yesterday, so I thought she might like me to take her to the pictures.

Lily, having heard the doorbell, skips downstairs and peeks around the kitchen wall. She can't see past her mother.

MOM

(Calling)

Lily. Someone's here to see you. A very dashing young man, if I may say so.

Lily sails around the corner and stops short.

LILY

Oh. It's you!

Bobby's face drops.

MOM

Give us a moment, Bobby.

Lily's mother lets the screen door swing shut. Bobby turns and sits down on the front step.

Honey—

LILY

Mom, I'm not going anywhere with Bobby. I couldn't. To be seen with Bobby—

MOM

I'm surprised. That's just how Michael treated you and you didn't like it very much.

Lily starts up the stairs.

But it's as you wish.

Mom turns back toward the front door.

Can't see the harm in an evening out, myself, and on such a nice night. Oo, but if you're going to be home, we could play cribbage. I'll tell him to be getting along—

LILY

I suppose I could give him a chance.

MOM

Well, I suppose.

Lily looks at Bobby on the step, picking at the bouquet of flowers.

MOM

Then shall I let him in?

Lily is all at once agitated.

LILY

Wait, I have to get ready. I can't go out like this.

Her mom suppresses a smile.

MOM

So run upstairs. He'll be here when you come down.

Lily nods and runs upstairs. Mrs. Price returns to the front door. She winks at Bobby.

Looks like you got yourself a date.

. . . . . .

Gabe is still standing on stage at the end of rehearsal. I go over to him since he seems to be waiting. Being around him makes me nervous, maybe because I still find the line between him and his character a little hazy. Maybe because he's always smiling and stands really close so that when I look up at him my chin practically rests on his chest. As it does now:

ME

Hey.

I am super-aware of the closeness. His T-shirt smells unexpectedly nice. When we're next to each other he has a good six inches on me and seems to enjoy it. I feel safe in scenes with him at least, like he won't forget the words because they're his own. But in these unscripted moments, I'm more nervous . . .

Case in point:

OUTSIDE PEELE'S. EARLY EVENING.

There's something about Gabe. He didn't ask me out like other people have, he kind of told me we had a date and I never corrected him. It's a refreshing change and even though I'm not sure it's a good idea, here I am! He swept me up in the idea, saying that it would help us get into character, which kind of makes sense. And with Ryan's comment in the hall, I didn't think it would hurt. Gabe met me after my shift, in a crisply pressed shirt—cute—and so far, I've had a surprisingly good time. You have karate tonight, so I haven't even had the chance to tell you I'm here with him yet. I have thought about Mia once or twice but otherwise I'm all here.

It's getting dark earlier, and fairy lights frame the windows of Peele's. Gabe is standing as close as usual and I can actually see the lights glinting in his eyes. As we walk, he's finding reason to be near me. He makes a joke *semi* at my expense so he can playfully push me and when I go flying he pulls me in toward him like a yo-yo. Aside from this athletic flirting, I like how I feel around him—girlish, desired, and I can't remember feeling that recently. The street is empty and the sun is setting so that everything glows amber. I'm thinking about making some comment about it but, when I turn around, he takes my face in his hands and kisses me! It's firm and warm. I think I make a small noise, more from surprise than enjoyment. Not that I'm not enjoying it but my heart isn't beating out of my chest as even my imagination can cause it to. There are no fireworks, no butterflies. It's nice but just not quite right. Putting my hands against his chest, I gently push away. He smiles.

GABE

Sorry, misread the moment maybe?

ME

Yep!

A semi-awkward, interesting pause.

Sorry. I like you, Gabe, and it's nice to have spent time together, but . . .

GABE

Say no more, babe.

There's the "babe" I was expecting!

ME

Really? So we're okay.

GABE

Sure.

That was easy. He's still relaxed, smiling! Maybe it's a girl thing to die of embarrassment after suddenly kissing someone. (And a normal thing!) Guys have it easy. When they're not embarrassed, it actually seems less embarrassing. *I kissed you. So what's the problem?* I feel a smile tug at the corner of my mouth as I imagine just kissing people when I wanted to. There'd be mayhem.

He's still gazing at me and I picture us silhouetted in the fading light. If only it was the most magical moment of my life. He looks like he might tuck a strand of hair behind my ear if one were going rogue but fortunately I'm uncharacteristically put together and he settles for running a fingertip under my chin.

GABE

I just looked at you, and the way you looked against the sunset, I knew I had to kiss you.

I'm torn between laughing out loud at the extreme schmaltz, and kissing him again. He hasn't stepped away and I wouldn't have to move far to be touching him. Part of me considers it: letting him press into me with his soft mouth and firm body, because he makes me feel sexy . . . feminine. But that's not a good enough reason.

ME

Sweet talk will get you nowhere, pal.

No one's said "pal" since the fifties but if he can get away with kissing me, I think I can get away with "pal." I push him to arm's length with a fingertip and then nudge him in the ribs with an elbow as we start walking, a nudge that says, "Ya big charmer, but enough of the kissing!" The gesture makes me think of you.

Gabe and I part company at the end of the street and he raises his hand in a farewell salute. Well, I didn't break his heart, I think as I walk away. I get the impression he was just trying it on and won't be crying into his pillow tonight.

......

MY BEDROOM. MIDNIGHT. THAT NIGHT.

I can't say the same for my good night's sleep. He kisses me, and I'm the one spending the rest of the night neuroticizing about it! We have to go back to rehearsals tomorrow and I hope it won't be weird. Especially with Mia there. I can't help wondering if I was clear enough that today is as far as it goes. Maybe I should have stepped back right away, not enjoyed the attention, the feel of him. I cover my face in the dark. I hope I didn't mess up.

Ten minutes later, the pendulum of my thoughts swings reassuringly to *no big deal*, he's hardly in love. Maybe, like me, there are people he'd rather be kissing. *Are* there people I'd rather be kissing? I think about Mia, nearly all the time, but thinking is one thing, kissing is another. I squeeze my eyes shut and give myself permission to fantasize. If Gabe can do *no big deal,* so can I. I try to imagine kissing Mia with my experimental new vibe. My imaginary self turns bright red and runs for the trees.

▪ ▪ ▪ ▪ ▪

REHEARSAL. SCHOOL THEATER. TWO DAYS LATER.

For some reason I haven't mentioned the Gabe thing to you yet. We didn't speak that night, and it would be strange to announce it out of the blue. Not that you're likely to ask, *Hey, kissed anyone today?* so I suppose I'll have to tell you if you're going to know.

To my great relief, rehearsals seem normal. As if he can hear my thoughts, Gabe, sitting across from me, winks. Mia notices and I blush. We haven't been acting as though it never happened. We're acting as though it happened and we have successfully put it behind us, which makes me feel spectacularly well-adjusted. If only we could all go around kissing people without detrimental effects. He's made jokes about it too, which helps. *I promise I won't kiss you,* he says when I get close enough. Maybe he's the kind of guy who kisses a lot of girls for no reason. Maybe I'm that kind of girl. I think not.

. . . . .

MY BEDROOM. THAT EVENING.

I'm getting ready to meet you at the movies. Kate is supposed to be coming with two of her friends. I'm running late—you're probably already there. Mom comes into my room with an armful of laundry. I catch a glimpse of the face she makes at the "interesting paint effect" every time she comes in. I can't find my shoes and it's driving me crazy. I'm worried we'll miss the beginning of the movie. Mom is speaking to me from the doorway.

MOM

I think it's exciting how much you're enjoying your theater class.

ME

Have you seen my shoes? I can't find them anywhere.

Mom points to a heap on the floor—her angle clearly advantageous. The mess has gotten away from me. She sits down on my bed.

MOM

And this play that you're a part of.

I try to zip up my sweater but it catches. The zipper is jammed. It won't go up or down. I can't go out with a jammed wonky sweater and I wail in frustration. Mom tells me to settle down and takes hold of my zip. It slides freely up to my neck and I wave as I run out of the room with a protracted *Bye* that comes with me down the stairs.

▪ ▪ ▪ ▪ ▪

MOVIE THEATER. SOON AFTER.

Skipping the last few feet to the doors of the movie theater, I see you up ahead in front of the movie posters, illuminated in the colored lights and turning your head with unnecessary regularity to look up and down the street, for me, I guess. I spring into your field of vision:

ME

Sorry I'm late.

You smile.

YOU

No probs.

ME

Where are the others?

YOU

Kate called. They can't make it. They're going to a later showing.

ME

Oh. We can go to a later one too, then—

YOU

Well, we're here now. Right?

ME

I guess.

And I follow you inside.

. . . . .

THE STREET. LATER THAT NIGHT.

We emerge back into the real world and walk in comfortable silence down the well-lit street away from the movie theater. My desire to be in movies is rekindled every time I see one. I want to be that girl: the girl kissed passionately after evil is vanquished, with fireworks and an orchestra, and it's everything she wants. Not the girl kissed without warning after her coffee-shop shift, with cake crumbs in her hair and an orange apron tucked over her arm. It seems like the perfect moment to mention Gabe, so even though I can't tell what's going through your head, I jump in:

ME

Gabe kissed me.

You turn and stare at me as if you expect me to continue, as if some kind of explanation for such a bewildering revelation will follow. You still have your 3-D glasses on and I almost laugh. You whip them off, your reaction intense, and I feel instantly defensive.

ME

There *are* people who might want to kiss me, you know.

YOU

Yeah, but I didn't know *you* wanted to kiss *him*.

I hold back my response. I can kiss anyone I choose. One kiss per annum doesn't seem so promiscuous to me but, feeling *surprisingly* vulnerable, I decide not to get into it.

ME

Well, then I'll hold off on having his babies!

I pretend to be amused by my humor. You don't.

YOU

I didn't see it coming, that's all.

Still cranky but you're trying.

ME

Neither did I!

Literally. We walk in silence.

I think I'll still have a run for my money
for biggest tramp in school.

You peer at me from the corner of your eye, the way you always do when you're about to give in.

YOU

Not a sure thing, maybe, but you definitely have a shot.

ME

Definitely!

I finally get a smile.

Well, I'm pretty sure it won't happen
again.

YOU

Pretty?

ME

Pretty definitely sure.

You seem almost appeased and let it go. I guess deep down I knew you'd be weird about it or I would have told you sooner. We get away with small talk for the rest of the walk home. You pause as we part company at your house.

YOU

Saturday's supposed to be warmer than usual. We should make the best of it.

ME

Sure.

YOU

So, I'll come by your house Saturday morning.

Good way to patch up this weirdness. You wave and leave me standing here, still thrown by your reaction to it all. I'm pretty sure we won't talk about the Gabe incident again.

▪ ▪ ▪ ▪ ▪

THEATER. THE NEXT DAY.

We've started rehearsals for the second half of the play. Even you're here today, finalizing lighting design, and I can see you settled in the third row. The rest of us are learning how to dance, fifties style, for a scene in act three. Gabe looks like he should be coordinated but he's struggling. He sways like he's playing dodgeball. Mia comes toward us, a soft maroon dress hugging her figure. (I'm almost tempted to revisit my "kiss without consequences" vibe.) I hope she'll reach for me but she pairs with Gabe, easing toward him to soften his posture. I hover, envious, until she remembers me. Then, as everyone else has been paired, she points me in the direction of the only person not already dancing. You. We grin awkwardly when you reach me onstage because of all the things we've done together through the years, slow dancing isn't one of them. Bouncing around like rock stars in my bedroom, maybe, but not this! A couple of people smile, seeing us deflect embarrassment with overzealous puppet sways. I spare another look, still tinged (*okay, saturated*) with envy, at Mia and Gabe over your shoulder, his hand on her waist and, with nothing left to do, we fit clumsily together. Right away, I feel my self-consciousness lift, surprised by how natural it feels. We turn smoothly together around the stage. Soon, caught up in the music, I forget how silly it is that it's you, and for a second, I even forget about Mia. I tip my head back, like ballroom dancers when they waltz, and we swoop giddily around the room, the music lifting my spirits until the lights above us spin and the room disappears and all I can hear is music and the sound of both of us laughing.

▪ ▪ ▪ ▪ ▪

MY BEDROOM. SATURDAY.

When I wake up, the sun is streaming through the gap in the curtain. It already feels warmer. The November breeze blows gently through the open window and I roll onto my side, stretching my arm out beside me. I look at my hand, spreading my fingers across the pillow. Still in the throes of sleep, and with faint memories of the remnants of a dream I was having, I touch my fingertips to the fabric, trying to remember what it had *just* felt like to believe it wasn't cotton beneath them. I close my eyes to hold on to the romanticized version of myself from my dream. Aware of my hair fanned across the pillow, my slip cool against my skin, I imagine how it will be to someday wake up beside someone, to feel an arm around my waist when I open my eyes. I tuck in my lower lip, thinking of how I want to look when I know someone is watching, and wondering if someone I want will ever be watching. Stretching, I open my eyes to the real world, slip sleepily out of bed, and blunder downstairs to make tea.

▪ ▪ ▪ ▪ ▪

THE KITCHEN. MOMENTS LATER.

I'm pressing down a piece of toast when I hear the bell. For some reason I'm not thinking about who it might be as I pad to the front door. I tug it open and take one look at you.

ME

Shit! Forgot.

It's Saturday and we made a plan. I don't know what happened, I just haven't thought of it since. We stare at each other.

ME

I can be ready in two minutes, I swear.

After another second, I realize why you might still be staring. When you used to spend the night when we were young, I was always in pink cotton pj's. Now, in my sexier days, my new satin slip probably comes as a surprise. It wouldn't have been my choice for company, even yours, and I check that you can't see more than you bargained for as you find your voice.

YOU

Two minutes?

It sounds like a challenge, with an edge that says I might have remembered if it had been more important to me. I see now how nicely dressed you are, with what looks like a picnic tucked under your arm. My toast pops. I turn and run up the stairs, wondering how high my slip rides up from your angle and, as if on cue, you call some quip about Gabe. When I'm tugging my slip off over my head in my bedroom I'm still thinking that Gabe was far from on my mind when I bought it.

So it took at least *three* minutes for me to find something to wear but when I reappear in jeans and a V-neck, you seem happy enough, sitting at the kitchen table and eating my toast.

You let me finish my tea before you stand up again.

YOU

Ready?

ME

Right behind you!

. . . . . .

THE STREET. SECONDS LATER.

The autumn sun is not yet overhead but it looks like you have something of a day planned. You're talking about taking a picnic up the hill this afternoon—to the highest point around. We used to sit there for hours when we were younger, lying on our backs on the grass on summer nights and looking at the sky. I'm only in a light jacket but it's warm enough for the day, and I wrapped a silk scarf around my neck on the way out the door. It makes me feel grown-up—it's just like one of Mia's. You seem intense today. Something's on your mind. Watching you from the corner of my eye, I get the impression that somehow this day started out more important to you than it did to me.

ME

You all right?

You give me a friendly nod, so I leave it at that.

We pass school on the way to the road up the hill and I skip ahead to the gate, feeling suddenly adventurous. I turn to see if you're feeling it too.

ME

Let's climb the gate like we used to.

Before we were in high school, we would climb over the gate during the summer to play football on the playing fields. We enacted whole sports events, and on this breezy Saturday *for old times' sake* appeals. Plus, being at school makes me feel close to Mia. Most people break out of school, not in, but I feel like peeking at the past from a complex present.

You look less enthused. I wrap my hands around the bars of the gate.

ME

Come on, we've done it before.

You shake your head, crushing my sense of adventure.

YOU

We shouldn't. We'll get in trouble.

Really?! *Trouble!*

And we kind of had a plan.

ME

A plan!

—I imitate, not completely unkindly, craving some spontaneity, and I reach for your hand but you ignore it.

YOU

First you forget—

I let my hand drop.

ME

I said I was sorry about that.

YOU

—And now you're acting like we don't already have something to do.

My urge to climb the gate and clear my head by tearing across the grass like we used to is a strong one, and I reach for you one more time but now you really pull back.

ME

You are so cautious, damn it. Just live a little!

I know right away I went too far. You're walking off. And for some reason, today, as if I haven't said enough, I keep talking.

ME

Look! If I'm pissing you off, at least stay and tell me so.

You spin around and I realize you're even angrier than I thought.

YOU

No, Phyre. Because then I might say something hurtful. Like *you* always do.

Stupefied pause. Like I *always* do. I stand uselessly, watching you walk away. This entire interlude has caught me off guard. I'm not even sure what I was pushing for, and now my heart feels heavy with guilt as you turn out of sight with your carefully packed picnic. How did this go *so* wrong *so* fast? I messed up today before it even started. We've never had a fight before this year, and now here's another. I feel a twist of unease in the pit of my stomach.

▪ ▪ ▪ ▪ ▪

MIA'S CLASSROOM. MONDAY. AFTER SCHOOL.

Mia, Kate, and I are here for a rehearsal after school. She suggested that the two of us explore emotion memory to help us relate to our characters. My heart shudders at even the idea of spending more time with the thoughts in my head. She sits on the desk in front of us. I look at her fingers curled around its edge and my mind swings from her soft skin to the way you walked away from me on Saturday. We haven't spoken since then. It's been harder to concentrate than I would have expected. My gaze returns to Mia's delicate wrists disappearing into her lilac shirtsleeves. She has patiently waited until she has my full attention.

MIA

Think of someone you have feelings for.

I look at her perfect face, flushing pink. She speaks more quietly than usual without the roomful of people to be heard over, leaning forward, swinging her legs thoughtfully.

MIA

Remember exactly how it feels to be around them.

Hot. Airless. Exhilarating. Cheeks burning, butterflies in my chest, and, underneath it all, pain.

Think of what you're self-conscious about when you want to impress them . . .

I steal a look at Kate. She's glowing with her own private thoughts of someone and I smile, feeling united by the feeling. I'm sure my own thoughts are playing across my face like a mini–projector screen. I wonder if Mia is thinking of someone, the same warmth spreading through her chest. She tucks her hair behind her ear. She *is* swept up in her own imagination. I watch the split second it takes for her to wet her lower lip before forming words.

MIA

. . . How it feels when they're close, if they touch your hand, catch your eye. How everything moves slowly around them but time goes so fast.

We sit in silence, thoughts playing behind our eyes. She's talking about my every moment around her. I try to imagine who she has felt this way about, and familiar envy seeps into my bloodstream. She has felt it, of course, everyone has, but I can't imagine anyone could make her feel as vulnerable as she makes me.

MIA

Every emotion you feel around someone you love is heightened.

My thoughts find their way back to you and our untouched picnic, and I realize how true it is. I'm closer to you than anyone else, and you're at the receiving end of every one of my emotions. When I look up, Mia is watching my projector-screen face. She smiles. I blush. Now all that registers on her face is an interest in the thoughts that she can see tinting my cheeks pink.

. . . . .

MY GARDEN. TUESDAY EVENING. 7 P.M.

I'm in a tree. You haven't spoken to me for a few days. I've sent you a gazillion messages but I can see it's going to take more. This is more. I'm sitting in our tree house, my arms wrapped around my knees, waiting. Waiting for you to follow the path of tea lights that I started at your front door, that lead all the way down the street to my house, down the path, through the garden, and around to the tree house: 708 of them! I've wrapped fairy lights around the tree trunk and draped them through the branches. And I'm sitting in the middle of it all. I've lined the perimeter of our makeshift tree house with tea lights too and have been hoping since I climbed up here half an hour ago that they won't make for a giant bonfire at any moment. Sitting in the middle of my own constellation, I can't imagine how I'll feel if you don't come. That would be a surefire way to humiliate me: make me blow out 708 tea lights. This evening you had a scholarship presentation at school so by my estimation you should just be home and following my twinkling path at this very moment. I strain to see the gate in the dark. Still no sign of you. Five minutes go by. I rest my chin on my knees, remembering the time I snuck into your room and released a jam jar of fireflies when you were asleep. When you woke up, we lay on your bed watching them light up the room. Then we couldn't get them to fly out the window and you were still seeing them days later. At night, they're magical but in the light they're just bugs. I hope this is more successful!

I'm starting to feel cramped and I'm thinking of all the reasons you might not come, all the reasons you might be home late, and my tea lights will be burned-out shells of liquid wax. I've just closed my eyes when I hear your voice:

YOU

You're a fire hazard!

I laugh, relieved. Happy.

ME

That's me. A Phyre Hazard.

I peer down and there you are, your head tipped back to look up at me, hands on your hips. You're all dressed up and you look perfect in my garden of lights, as if you've put on your best outfit just to walk a twinkling path made in your honor, your own red carpet. My "Sorry" speech has gone out of my head so I go with the short version as I reach out and pull you up into the tree beside me, trying not to set you on fire.

ME

Sorry I'm an ass.

YOU

Me too.

I laugh again, heartily, elbowing you gently, but you make a show of nearly falling out of the tree anyway. I reach for your arm and keep hold.

ME

Missed you.

YOU

You did?

And that's it. We're just you and me again.

. . . . . .

THEATER. AFTER SCHOOL. TWO WEEKS LATER.

The weeks, crammed with rehearsals, are flying by. We've spent the afternoon watching in awe as the set has been built. According to Kate, Mia had her heart set on the play despite the complex set, so she brought in a friend: a handsome guy, not much older than she is—annoyingly handsome, the kind of guy described in books as "flashing a smile." She's been conferring with him attentively for most of the afternoon. Kate has been flirting. He doesn't seem to mind but he talks to us like we're kids and it reminds me how much respect we get from Mia. Kate stands beside me on the balcony above him (believe me when I say that a plumber's crack isn't flattering on anyone) as he straightens up and slips his screwdriver into his tool belt.

MR. HANDSOME

All right, girls? You be careful up there.

Kate and I look at each other but my look says "urgh" and her look says "dreamy!" Flashing a smile, Mr. Handsome joins Mia, who is waiting at the door of the auditorium, and puts his hand on the small of her back (double "urgh") as they walk out. I catch your eye, looking up at us from ground level and I do an impression of him. Loading my imaginary tool belt like a gun into a holster, I do my best Wild West walk and blow the smoke from my fingertips before giving you a wink and a finger point.

KATE

Are you crazy, he was gorgeous!

ME

Yeah, and he thought so.

I picture again the way he ushered Mia from the theater before my attention returns to the upside. I look down at his handiwork from above, and it is amazing. Beneath us, for the second half of the play, he's set a swimming pool into the raised stage. The removable floorboards of the Price house come up and this tank will be a glistening pool. The staircase to Lily's bedroom in the first half becomes the balcony over the swimming pool. We've been appointed the task of set painting for the rest of the afternoon—a forte of yours rather than mine—so here we are.

I've started on the shutters on the upstairs windows. Below me, you and Kate are painting the French doors. I'm trying to create the effect of slats on my shutter with a second shade of green as I catch snippets of your conversation. Kate is talking about a guy she's seeing. *He's in twelfth grade and really hot*—she hasn't mentioned smart. Now she's asking you. You're mumbling something. I pause to hear better, as if my brushstrokes make too much noise. You haven't mentioned anyone to me, and I've asked a million times! Why wouldn't you talk to me if you liked someone? I can keep secrets too. I stick my head over the balcony to glare at you but you're not looking. My glare goes unnoticed and Kate is busy admiring her work. I go back to my shutter, my attention to detail getting hazier by the minute. Next thing I know, you're beside me. I pretend not to see you at first, tilting my head to evaluate my work. Then I huff.

ME

This looks like crap!

You smile.

You're not supposed to agree.

YOU

Here.

You take the brush from my hand and add a few choice lines of darker shadow. Miraculously, it already looks more like a shutter. I take the paintbrush back and sweep a thin streak across your cheek.

ME

Thanks, I was just getting to that!

I turn away triumphantly. Greeted by too long a silence, I peer back at you. You've pressed your entire palm into my palette of paint and are coming toward me. Shrieking, I run for it.

. . . . .

THEATER COURTYARD. AFTERNOON. THE NEXT DAY.

The rehearsal schedule for today lists my scene with Gabe near the end of play. Mia and I are alone, waiting in the theater courtyard. We're here under the sky because the scene is outdoors and Mia says we should rehearse in an open space. We're sitting on the wall beneath the arch. Gabe is fifteen minutes late. She looks over her shoulder for him, and I watch the tendons spring in her graceful neck. She hops down off the wall.

MIA

Well, as you've taken the time to be here, let's rehearse.

I look at her, filled with nerves. The sun has come out between the treetops behind her, giving her a halo-like glow. I stand up and we move beneath the evergreen laurel trees lining the path. The undersides of the leaves are so peaceful, pale and vulnerable like the belly of a tortoise.

Standing face-to-face in the dappled light, we are closer together than ever before. I can see her necklace at her open collar. I have never seen it this close and she notices me looking.

MIA

Cassiopeia.

I meet her eyes.

My necklace.

She clasps it delicately between finger and thumb, and I feel the thrill of being let in on something personal.

ME

Where did you get it?

MIA

It was a gift.

She doesn't say who from, but I'm guessing *boyfriend*. I step even closer.

ME

Can I see?

She nods and raises her chin. She lets go before I have the necklace properly between my fingers, giving me the chance to lift it gently from the notch in her collarbone where it falls. I realize with a quickening pulse that it's the first time I've touched her. I tilt the tiny constellation to look at it in the sunlight, a delicate twist of silver.

MIA

She was beautiful and vain, Cassiopeia.

ME

So nothing like you. I mean, not vain.

Help. I think I just called her beautiful!

MIA

Nothing like me—

—She smiles.

I wear it as a reminder that vanity can
be a downfall.

I nod my head wisely, then speak entirely without thinking.

ME

I have a Cassiopeia in freckles.

MIA

You do?

I'm still holding her necklace so she can't move away but she doesn't seem to mind. My skin is mostly clear so I've always thought it funny that five freckles should arrange themselves exactly like a constellation. I come to my senses and let the necklace rest back against her neck.

MIA

Can I see?

I hesitate, wondering why in the world I mentioned it.

ME

Oh, it's on my body—I mean, not immediately visible.

Left to the imagination it's just sounding worse so I realize it's probably better to show her. I carefully lift my shirt—hoping my slim-cut jeans are doing me justice—and on my left side is the small and exact replica of the "W." She looks closer.

MIA

That's amazing. Perfect alignment!

She can't see my nod as her face is inches from my body.

ME

Best yet, I don't need a necklace to be reminded of the perils of vanity.

She laughs, and I almost stop breathing. I'm so aware of her. Can she feel how aware I am? She has to. I can almost see the tentacles of blue electricity flaring off my body and reaching for her, like the globes in science. She straightens up, still smiling, and it takes me a second to realize I haven't let go of my shirt. Now I'm just voluntarily holding it in the air! I quickly smooth it back into place, feeling ridiculous. I fill the millisecond of silence.

ME

So there we go!

She brings us coolly back to the play with a comment about Lily's vanity masking her insecurity, and we run through the scene. Mia turns to me thoughtfully at the end.

MIA

What's she really saying here?

My senses are working overtime, I can feel everything. The ground beneath my feet. Gravity. The breeze. The sun filtering through the trees. Mia's gaze.

ME

She's trying to give the impression that she doesn't have feelings for him. She'd never want him to know. I'm not sure she even fully admits it to herself. But there's a part of her that has to accept it. She loves him, and she wishes she could take a chance, that he feels it too.

She smiles.

MIA

Good. So, say the lines as if you want him to believe them but remember that we can't ever help giving away a little of how we really feel.

When we play the scene again, I give myself the freedom to say everything I've wanted to. The words are the same but I stop repressing every self-conscious gesture that gives me away. I let my eyes express what I pretend not to feel at every moment. When we reach the end of the scene, she nods, suspended, engaged. And in that second, I wish she knew everything that I feel. She smiles breezily.

MIA

Excellent! See how interesting it becomes?

As she turns away, I reach out and touch her arm. She looks back at me, her eyes wider than usual, waiting for me to say something. I don't speak. I haven't thought of what I would say.

MIA

Phy?

My hand is still on her arm. I search for words to go with the gesture. After a second, she puts her hand gently over mine, moving it from her arm, but holding it warmly for a second.

MIA

You okay?

ME

Yeah. Fine. I . . . Thanks, for your help.

MIA

Need a ride home?

. . . . .

MAIN SCHOOL HALLWAY. SOON AFTER.

We stop by the teachers' lounge so she can pick up her bag. *I'll just be a minute,* she says, smiling over her shoulder as she pushes open the door. I peer after her into the empty room: the view from the door, the only view I've ever had. I picture the other side that I'll never see. A place becomes so much more fascinating when you can't go in. Then you have to imagine it. I'm sure that imagining is sometimes a lot more exciting than the reality. The hall is deserted and the door is still open a crack. I wonder what she would do if I just followed her in. There's nothing to stop me, just the little voice in my head reminding me I am *not supposed to.* I wonder how different I would be in a world with no consequences. Will the voice telling me what's right always be so loud? I'm still wondering when she reappears, her bag over her shoulder, and we head toward the gate.

▪ ▪ ▪ ▪ ▪

THE ROAD. LATE AFTERNOON.

Watching the trees rush by behind her, I wonder how vividly I'll be able to relive this moment—if I'll be able to remember exactly how I feel *right here, right now.* I lean against the window of Mia's car, my head turned so I can look at her. Cassiopeia twinkles in the light. The golden afternoon sun makes her narrow her eyes sleepily against the glow, and in the unfiltered light her white shirt is semitranslucent. From this angle, I can see the length of her collarbone to the curve of her shoulder. Music is playing quietly on the radio. There's no need to talk. She sees me watching her and smiles with sincerity. Being with her makes me feel like an adult, like we're stealing away together. Seeing the blur of streets go by, I imagine the possibility that she won't take me home. That she'll keep going. She'll drive away with me to a place where we can be together and she can tell me how she really feels. So soon, it seems, she pulls over in front of my house. She'll be gone in a minute, it's happened too fast. I sit in the car for a moment, and when she looks at me again, I don't look away. Shall I tell her I love her? Mom waves from the window. Mia waves back warmly.

Standing at the curb, I stoop to say my thanks through the open window, and in the cover of a blinding sunset, I watch the taillights of the car pull away. I wonder for a second if she's watching me in the rearview mirror. Blinking away the sun spots from my eyes, I walk up the path to the front door with one thought. Mia knows where I live. I'll feel differently every time the doorbell rings because of the new 1 percent chance it could be her.

. . . . . .

MY BEDROOM. THAT EVENING.

I flop onto my bed. My heart is still somewhere between the drive home and the rehearsal under the trees. I close my eyes to imagine my way back there, like when you wake up from the perfect dream and squeeze away awake in favor of asleep. The phone rings—I pick it up and it's you. *Hey,* I sing, lightness and heaviness balled up together in my heart so it doesn't know whether to sink or float. *Hey,* you say, with less enthusiasm. I sit up:

ME

What's wrong?

Check the school website, you say. Check Got Gossip. So I do, fingers shaking. I click on the header, apprehension flooding my body. My breath stops in my throat and I feel sick. The page shows a photograph, of me. A photograph of this afternoon. *Mia on Phyre?* I can barely bring myself to read on.

> A certain ex-hot-lister seen here
> wrapped up in private drama with her
> very own teacher: new flame or is
> Phyre just carrying a torch for her?
> Can the heat be sustained? Check
> back for more.

I stare at the screen, wondering whether I'll die so I won't have to go to school tomorrow. For a second, it seems like nothing will ever be the same. We're standing so close in the photograph, in the shadow of the trees, my hand reaching for her. She's just a shape in the foreground but it's as if the camera has captured every ounce of my longing. Reddening with anger and embarrassment, I fight a sudden pang of isolation. Can they really do that? I've been so careful not to give anything away and in the single moment that I let it show, *snap*.

. . . . . .

SCHOOL GATE. THE NEXT MORNING.

I couldn't sleep. I lay awake for most of the night wondering if I could ever come to school again. My half-awake, half-asleep dreams played out the day ahead, with people staring and pointing, and now I have to go through it all for real. From the gate, the path to the steps has never looked so long. I dressed in black this morning, resigned. People take strength from other people being targets; it means they're not at the bottom of the heap. I've been staring at the path for a full minute before I notice that you're beside me. I smile a halfhearted "thanks for waiting"—you could have gone ahead to avoid being seen with me. People don't look too menacing from here but I'm sure that when I start to weave between groups, they'll notice me.

I take a falsely confident step toward school and the wave of fear I experience cements my decision to hide behind the gate until everyone has started to move inside. We stand side by side in silence as the figures flock through the doors into school. I take a deep breath, and we make our move. Despite everything, it looks like you've decided to try to make me laugh. You're crouching beside the wall and have signaled, spy style, that you'll move out first. Sure enough, imaginary gun drawn, you've just darted through the gate and disappeared. After a moment, you appear around the wall and beckon me to follow, taking cover behind one of the big maples. With my life at an end, good luck getting even a smile out of me. But I have to make it through the day somehow so I reach you at the tree and we peer around it to see the crowd at the door thinning. You're standing straight as an arrow against the tree and you tug me behind it when I stray. I carefully take the two fingers that you were using for pretend firepower and press them to my temple. You frown and brush them gently against my cheek instead but just for a heartbeat. We stand quite still, without speaking, as if spy rules prohibit it. I think for a minute you might say something about this mess but then you look toward school and motion the all clear.

. . . . . .

SCHOOL HALLWAY. TEN MINUTES LATER.

We're running the gauntlet. There was no way to avoid the hallways without going into class late, and then everyone would really stare. So far, it's like my fitful dreams—people staring with varying degrees of subtlety—and someone just whistled! Even my nightmares didn't account for whistling. Now completely unable to pretend it's my imagination, I panic and want to run. You sense my flight instinct and catch me by the arm so I can't. Thanks to you, I make it to homeroom with tingling fingers and no blood below the elbow but without the added humiliation of being *the girl who ran through school.*

. . . . .

HOMEROOM. SOON AFTER.

I'm curled in a chair in homeroom. First period starts any minute but I can't bring myself to go. I shouldn't have come to school at all. You kneel down in front of me.

YOU

Hey, Phyre Hazard. Don't let them bring you down.

I stare. You start to stand with fake resignation—at least I hope it's fake.

Well, hey, you gave it your best! Nice knowing you. Let me know if you need help crawling into a hole.

Even crawling into a hole does sound effortful right now. I grab hold of your sleeve and you meet my eyes with all the sensitivity you have left.

ME

That'd be great.

As I follow you out of the room, I remember that we have Mia second period. I'm not sure if that's a good thing or not but if I can talk to her maybe I'll stay sane.

. . . . . .

MIA'S CLASSROOM. SECOND PERIOD.

I'm sitting with my eyes on the door. Mia's not here yet and every moment I'm an easy target. I've moved to a seat at the back of class so I can't feel the eyes like lasers burning holes in my back. No one has said anything yet—their looks say enough. The door opens. Mrs. Keen! It's Mrs. Keen with a stack of papers. I almost stand up and yell at her to leave. Where's Mia?

MRS. KEEN

Settle down, everyone. I'm covering this morning, so you can use this as a reading period. Miss Quin says there's plenty to do.

I shift in my chair, feeling heat rush to my face. I can't begin to read, I'll go crazy. That hole is sounding better and better. I see you looking at me and wait for the blood to stop rushing through my temples before I meet your gaze. There isn't much you can do from where you are; I have to survive this by myself. I take shallow breaths. I can make it through this day.

. . . . . .

LUNCH.

To make that just a tad more difficult, earlier I saw someone who I don't even know open a text message and look directly at me. I didn't stick around long enough to find out why but, as I'm walking down the hall at lunch, I pass a gaggle of girls and get a pretty good impression over a ninth grader's shoulder. There's the picture, smaller, thank God, but recognizable, being sent around cell phones. The bravest kind of bullying! Pressing buttons and never even looking the person in the eye. I'd rather it still be like kindergarten, so when someone snatches something from you, you can thump them and then burst into tears. Even on a one-inch screen I can see the picture all too clearly. Terrific. My reputation as the crazy-infatuation girl is taking shape. Ryan catches my eye across the hallway, a corner of his mouth turning up as if to say *Ah, that explains it!* If I were any closer, I'd hit him.

. . . . .

FRONT STEPS. AFTER SCHOOL.

Finally, finally, the end is in sight. I bolt out of biology to find you waiting at the steps. All the air inside me is just bursting to escape. You're standing beside your bike, which I didn't see this morning. Looks like you knew I would need a quick getaway. Relieved, and feeling the threat of tears swelling in my throat, I climb onto the crossbar and tuck up my knees.

YOU

Ready?

More people are streaming from the front doors of school and I call to you as if you're a mile away.

ME

Go!

We pull away and from the first turn I know where you're taking me. The weather has darkened and heavy clouds have blackened the sky. The trees meet overhead, making a tunnel of this stretch of road. On sunny days there is perfect dappled light but today even the weather knows to be bleak and heavy. I plead with myself not to take the easy road—to deny it, to shout from the rooftops that it isn't true that I care about Mia, just to be the same as everyone else. I can be brave. Feeling the wind against my face, I'm saved by the shadows of the trees. I feel you behind me, standing up, pressing into the pedals as we climb uphill. You power us forward, the dimness getting thicker and thicker as we leave town behind us. We come out of the trees, and when we reach the top of the hill, you stop, barely out of breath. I jump down. Here, at the highest point for miles, where it is always blustery and no one can hear me, I cry into the wind. And it's not pretty-girl crying. We stand side by side. You take my hand and hold tight, as if I'm hanging from a bridge and you're all that's holding me up.

. . . . .

MY KITCHEN. LATER.

Mom is at the sink, washing a teacup when I come in. I blink in the light.

MOM

Phy, hon, you okay?

ME

Mm–hmm.

I'm spectacularly unconvincing. I feel the prickle of tears again and even though I'm grateful she always notices when something's wrong, I head for my room.

MOM

Sit down for a minute. Can I tell you a secret?

I turn back and flop down at the kitchen table. Mom comes over and scoots a chair in beside me.

MOM

Before I was your mother, I was a teenager.

I smile for the first time today.

ME

Ha-ha!

MOM

Strange but true. When things went wrong, it felt like the world would end. But it never did. Now, I can't even remember what those things were. It doesn't make whatever *this* is less upsetting, but trust me that someday you'll have a new perspective. It's only as important as you let it be.

She smiles and I love her for trying.

There was this guy I liked in school. He asked me to the dance, and I was thrilled—spent hours picturing every moment. That night, he kissed my best friend, Sophie Vargas. She was gorgeous but already had a date and it seems he just needed an in.

ME

Oh, Mom!

She nods and all of a sudden I can see her at my age.

I thought you said you couldn't remember any of those things!

MOM

So, there are some you never forget. But I survived, didn't I?

As she gets up, I realize that she helped me think about something else for thirty seconds. And yet I'm quite sure that this is one I'll never forget.

▪ ▪ ▪ ▪ ▪

THE NEXT DAY. (THREE HOURS OF SLEEP LATER.)

We pass Mia's room first thing. I have an overwhelming desire to see her. Her door is open a crack and there is a sliver of sun across the hallway. There are voices. Two, and I'd know hers anywhere. Thank God she's here today. I press my face to the crack to see what's happening. Mia is standing behind her desk. The second voice is the department head. Footsteps come toward me, bringing her imposing shadow closer, and the door pushes shut. The sun's gone. Mia is in trouble and it's my fault.

. . . . . .

SCHOOL SWIMMING POOL. FIRST BREAK.

If yesterday felt slow, this morning seemed to stop. Finally, I'm here waiting for a rehearsal with Mia. I'm terrified that she won't show up or that she'll be somehow changed.

Relief courses through my body as I see her round the corner. From here she has her usual serene expression, so not everything can be different. She smiles as she reaches me and, despite everything, I feel the same as always when I look at her.

. . . . . .

POOLSIDE. SOON AFTER.

In my bathing suit, clutching my towel around me, I'm staring into the still, green-blue water, semi-naked in front of the one person who has turned my world upside down—not feeling remotely vulnerable or anything! I kneel down to feel the water and gaze at the rippling shape of my reflection. Mia appears beside me. We still haven't really spoken, I can't find the courage. I slip into the deep end of the pool and cling to the side. When I look up at her, this, for some reason, strikes me as the last moment I can bear to leave everything unsaid.

ME

Did you see it?

MIA

See what?

I feel so small beneath her. She kneels at the side of the pool in front of me.

ME

The picture!

MIA

Yes, I saw that.

Her tone is still calm.

But Phy—

She holds on to my forearms, looking into my troubled eyes.

Try not to care so much what people think.

Not care? Ha! I blink.

ME

And you're not in trouble?

MIA

Why would I be in trouble?

This makes sense to me now. I struggle to make sense of the rest of my jumbled thoughts.

ME

When you weren't here yesterday . . .

MIA

Oh . . . I had an interview . . . I've got a new full-time teaching position for next semester.

She is clearly minimizing her excitement for my sake. I swallow.

ME

That's great.

For a moment everything seems so normal, except for me. I feel like I've been spinning out of control all by myself. I press my face against my arm and take a breath.

MIA

Ready?

Pushing away from the wall, I nod and sink into the water. Opening my eyes and looking up at the surface, I see Mia's outline, kneeling at the side and shimmering. I sink deeper, feeling the pressure increase and wondering how I possibly got to this point. I swim away along the bottom of the pool and back. My lungs are bursting but I would stay down here forever if I could. After another thirty seconds, I start rising to the surface against my will. Mia reaches into the water and brings me gently into the air, supporting my chin on the surface. I float there. She smiles.

MIA

Yes, I think you're ready.

. . . . .

SCHOOL LIBRARY. BREAK. THE NEXT DAY.

I'm hiding: sitting at the window and watching people collect in the courtyard below—still avoiding public places. Silence sounds louder in a big room because it echoes back at you. I rest my forehead against my hand as the sun comes out and casts a long window-shaped shadow across the table in front of me. It's strangely peaceful. Looking down, I notice Cara's face, amid a group of people, turned up to my window and I meet her gaze. Almost immediately she disappears from sight. I'm not surprised to see her at the top of the library stairs moments later. She makes no effort to be quiet.

CARA

Hey, rock star. Why are you hiding up here?

ME

You didn't see the site?

CARA

Are you kidding? Sure I did. I'd be out there taking a bow.

This is a genuinely befuddling moment.

ME

Why?

CARA

You scored a hottie. So what's the problem?

She is so matter-of-fact I almost can't help agreeing. I don't even see the need to set her straight.

But sure, be like everyone else. See if I care.

She smiles and, for the first time since all this happened, I actually do feel normal. She turns toward the door.

CARA

Are you coming?

I hesitate, glancing out the window at the pack of people.

Come on. They're probably just jealous. And you can't stay in here forever.

ME

I figured I could at least sit here until this class graduates.

CARA

You'd get hungry.

She smiles again. Perspective. I think of Mia and everything I'm hiding from. Sitting here isn't going to solve any of it. I push back my chair—the screech deafening in the silence—and I follow Cara out into the sun.

. . . . . .

SCHOOL COURTYARD. MINUTES LATER.

Cara gives my arm a reassuring squeeze and I cross the courtyard toward you. I am a sitting duck, the bobbing downy underside before it gets swallowed by a crocodile, leaving a single floating feather on the surface of the water. Grace looks over. Her eyeliner today is almost raccoon-like.

GRACE

Hey, Phyre. You didn't mind about the picture, did you?

Me? Mind? No!

We were just messing around.

And it was hysterical! I bite my lip and smile, as she seems halfway genuine. She babbles on, then rests her forearm on my shoulder. I cover my surprise with a sound a horse might make. I consider pretending to go with this, to play at being jovial as if the whole thing has amused me, but I don't see why I should pretend that it's all fine. I stand as casually as I know how for about thirty seconds, and then I press a decisive fist to your arm and start toward the door. We walk.

As we reach the hallway, you break into a smile, a partial celebration of my survival and, partly, I can tell, residual amusement at the sounds I make when under pressure. You used to name them: angry hippo, confused parrot. This time, I let it slide. You're one of the few people I let laugh at me, and only sometimes! Hands in my pockets, chin to my chest, I peer at you. You let yourself look happy for the first time today. After a minute, your focus shifts past me to the wall, and I look too. It's a poster for the play; they're pinned up all around school. It looks like a 1950s movie poster, my silhouette in profile, and the caption: *Will she recognize true love before it's too late?*

YOU

Looks good!

You smile.

You look good.

I smile.

ME

Thanks.

We stand in silence for another moment and I realize how lucky I am to have someone I can be myself around, in all my melancholy glory. The bell goes. I sigh.

Well, gotta get my books for class.

YOU

Okeydoke!

This time, my smile trumps my impulse to cringe. Despite all this, you made me smile. And here in the hallway, tired of this seriousness, everything suddenly strikes me as funny.

ME

Okeydoke!

Pathetically funny but it's a relief to laugh, and I do. Helplessly, for the first time in days. I laugh so much I have tears running down my face, till my stomach hurts and I'm gasping for air. You laugh too but instead of your laughter being tinged with hysteria, it's tinged with sympathy. You give me a hug.

YOU

Hey, you want help with the swimming-pool scene for the play? We could practice on the weekend.

ME

Sure.

And as we walk, I feel almost upbeat.

■ ■ ■ ■ ■ ■

NEIGHBORS' SWIMMING POOL. SATURDAY AFTERNOON.

We can't use the school pool because it's the weekend, so we're over at your neighbors'. They have the nice house next to yours and a pool—outdoors, but heated. It's late afternoon already, so the underwater lights are on, making it glow a brilliant blue. I sink into the warm water. It's colder out than in, steam rising off the surface, evaporating where it meets the cold air. We duck under together, gliding along the bottom of the pool. You've always been comfortable in water—graceful and quick. I roll over to look up at the surface, to make sure I'm not causing ripples. It's like a different world down here, the surface like a sheet of glass above us. You swim ahead, light glancing off your body. You come up in the shallow end and I swim up to you, wrapping my arms around your knees and tipping you into the water. We break into the air together laughing. I push my hair back from my face. The sun has disappeared behind the trees and I hear you sigh in the silence. You sink down into the water again, resting your chin on the surface like me, to keep your shoulders warm. I suck in the brisk air. I feel alive, divided in two, my body relaxed, soaked in warmth, my face wide awake in the cold air. I watch the tips of my hair fan out on the surface, thinking of all the times we've gone swimming together since we were young. We bob there a while longer, just breathing and listening to the birds that sing at dusk. Under the water, your skin appears almost blue in the light, separate from the tops of your tanned shoulders. Now and again I duck beneath the surface to warm up my face. Only when I finally start to shiver do we make a run for our towels, the cold air catching in my throat until I'm hugging my towel around me.

. . . . . .

YOUR BEDROOM. SOON AFTER.

We watch the last of the light drain out of the sky from the warmth of your window. Kneeling on your bed to see over your head into the small mirror, I pin up my hair, mumbling through the clips in my mouth.

ME

Anks er elppin me.

You turn around and gently remove the clips so I can smile at you for real.

YOU

Hope you didn't say something really special 'cause I missed it.

ME

I said, *anks*.

You laugh the warmest laugh you have.

YOU

In that case, you're *wecom*.

You kneel beside me, your face still glowing from the cold. Mine must be too because you run your finger down my nose, then drop abruptly back on to the bed. I look at my cherry-pink nose in the mirror and cover it with my hand, pulling my sweater up to rest below my eyes. When you catch my eye, you laugh again.

ME

I'd never have made it through this week without you.

As I watch you tug your fingers through your hair, I think about how self-involved I've been. With everything that's been going on, I can't remember the last time I asked about you.

ME

How are you?

You reach out a hand for me to shake.

YOU

I'm fine, thanks. How are you?

I slap your hand away.

ME

Stop, I'm serious! I haven't asked in a long time and I'd like to know.

You pull your sweater up over your nose too so I can only see your eyes, your blond hair drying in a flighty sweep across your forehead.

YOU

Everything's good. Really good.

ME

And you would tell me if it wasn't?

YOU

Sure I would.

Your eyes crease, so I figure you're smiling.

Feel ready for the play?

I look right at the dark centers of your eyes, the only feature I can see.

ME

I think so.

. . . . . .

THEATER. AFTERNOON OF DRESS REHEARSAL. THE NEXT THURSDAY, BEFORE FIRST NIGHT.

I'm sitting at the edge of the glistening pool of water in the stage, knees tucked up and gazing at the shimmering surface beneath the stage lights. There are a few people spread around the theater, putting finishing touches to the set and lighting. I'm trying not to look at Mia. I can sense her standing in the first row and looking out at the stage but I figure that if I seem aloof I'll prove something to the rest of the cast and to myself. I'm not sure she's even noticed. There's no heart-break, no *Phyre, I feel like you're not speaking to me.* Besides, ignoring her is not helping. The whispering has continued. I take a breath. It's almost the end of the semes-ter, nearly the holidays, and she'll be gone. Bittersweet. Maybe I'll be able to get on with my life.

We have the dress rehearsal tonight. I shall immerse myself in Lily's life, or try. Seeing you at the top of the auditorium steps brings me quickly back to myself. I watch you focusing a spotlight on the balcony above me, your concentration lapsing into laughter as I notice Kate's arms wrapped around your knees to keep you stable.

I turn instead and watch the ripples of light dancing on the cyclorama behind me. After a few minutes, a silhouette steps into the picture, a fan of shadows, one strong with fuzzy impersonators from all the lights overhead. I pause, my space shared. Mia?—the shadow of a gesture I'd know anywhere—better, it's you. I turn. Your hair is still sliding back into place from you running your fingers through it. But you're not looking at me, you're gazing up at the balcony. Light spills through the windows, as if we're outside looking in. A spotlight swings across the stage, catching you in its beam and I look past you to Kate at the lighting rig. You, never in the spotlight, are illuminated by its cool glow. Standing center stage, you bring up your right hand and the spotlight's focus softens, your shadow fanning out around you. You gesture with the other hand and the auditorium lights go down, leaving us in the dark except for the light from the house and from the balcony, glowing by lantern and moonlight.

Noticing me now as if for the first time you beckon and I follow you up the stairs to the balcony. You set me in place and step back to scrutinize me.

YOU

Bring up the moon!

The cool light brightens, giving the side of your face a bluer hue against the golden glow of the lights from the windows. And then you smile, your green eyes glinting.

YOU

Don't ever say I didn't give you the moon.

The people in the theater seem to have thinned out. I can't see anyone, not even Mia, and it feels as if we're alone. We stand here in the quiet, your eyes still on me, but the big picture is clearly all you're thinking about as you disappear abruptly back down the stairs, leaving me alone on the balcony. I squint into the darkness. I can't see more than a few signs of movement, and I hear you with Kate up at the lighting rig. Then your voice out of the darkness:

YOU

Thanks, Phy.

And that's it. I stand on the balcony for another moment looking out at nothing. I can still hear your voices, hushed voices that carry like the hiss of a whisper. I know that feeling. I'm jealous. Feeling exposed today for all the wrong reasons, in a shining pool of light that isolates me from everyone else, I head quickly down the stairs and escape behind the curtain into the wings. I pause in the darkness, safe and invisible. I'm not sure how many minutes I've stood here when I hear footsteps coming down the aisle toward the stage. There's a voice. Kate's:

KATE

. . . It's always nice when someone tells you they like you.

I put my face instantly to the gap in the curtain. The stage lights illuminate the space in front of the first row where she's standing, with *you*. You like Kate? That's impossible! She can't mean you. You would have told me that! But you haven't. Have you confided in *her* about someone, and not in me? She swings her hair intimately over her shoulder—no hands, just a swish of her head, which is ridiculous! I fight my childish impulse to jump out and yell aha—the vindictive "I know all your little secrets" kind of yell.

KATE

So, what's the plan for tonight?

You have a plan for tonight? You're heading out of my line of sight. There's nothing I can do without sending a great big ripple down the entire curtain if I touch it. Your voices move toward the door.

YOU

I figured we could celebrate opening night somehow. A good-luck thing. Seems like a decent reason . . .

I push through the curtain, incredulous that you could do this without me. You both turn. You have your "I'm hiding something" face—I've never been on the receiving end of it. I've only ever seen it from the corner of my eye when we're side by side and my expression matches. You're still looking a little stricken as Kate clasps your shoulder and makes a hasty exit:

KATE

See ya.

We stare at each other.

ME

Shouldn't you catch up? Sounds like you have something fun planned.

A snide tone hampers my plan to be mature. I give an artificial sigh.

Well, I'll be glad to head home and get a good night's sleep before tomorrow. Is that the best idea, to go out tonight? See you bright and early.

Surprise gone, now you just look offended.

YOU

Phyre, I was talking about you.

Huh?

I'd been telling Kate I wanted to do something for you before your first night . . . But we don't have to if you think it's stupid. I just thought it would be nice, because this thing's been so important to you.

Three-minute pause.

ME

Oh.

The genius strikes again.

I thought you were making plans with Kate.

The only thing worse than eavesdropping is eavesdropping badly and misunderstanding. You shake your head.

ME

You *said* "we."

YOU

We, you and me.

ME

When you're talking to someone, *we* usually means *we*.

I gesture with big circling arms.

YOU

When *I* say we, I usually mean us.

ME

That's not normal!

YOU

You know, you can be pretty hard to please.

Silence.

ME

I only said it was stupid because I thought you hadn't included me.

Your sigh is genuine. Not my best moment. We walk slowly toward the door.

ME

Is there any chance I can make up for this one on a quicker schedule? Because I'd really like to be talking by tomorrow night.

YOU

Admitting you're crazy is a good first step.

ME

First step. Check.

I check it off with a finger in the air. There's no coming back from this in a hurry, so I give your hand a squeeze and let you go.

. . . . .

FIRST NIGHT. HAIR AND MAKEUP. CURTAIN UP: FIFTY MINUTES.

Eyes closed, I sit in costume in front of the mirror. I can sense people rushing past. Their voices seem hollow and far away. My heart has been beating out of my chest all day but now that evening is here, I'm almost calm. I can feel on my eyelids the light touch of Viv, who is in charge of hair and makeup, sweeping on eye shadow. I sit still, playing with the tiny buttons at the wrists of my gloves. We always have a purpose, I think to myself. I wanted to be Lily to impress Mia. Tonight, I want to be Lily for me. I feel the tug of a curling iron and smell hair spray. Viv is in front of me now, blocking the bulbs around the mirror from making the inside of my eyelids glow. When I sense her step away, I open my eyes and the room comes rushing back. I look at my reflection for the first time. But it's not me I see, it's Lily. I take a deep breath. I wonder if this really will all seem unimportant some day. It feels important today.

. . . . .

DRESSING ROOM. CURTAIN UP: THIRTY-FIVE MINUTES.

I walk back into the dressing room to warm up and my heart leaps to see a bunch of red daisies on the table. There's a note. I pick it up. *Knock 'em dead.* I hear someone in the hall behind me and instinctively scrunch the note into a ball. A rumor about notes from Mia is the last thing I need. I glance over my shoulder. The door doesn't open and I look back at the crumpled paper in my hand. I try instantly to flatten out the crumple but it's not the same. The flowers will die! The note I could have kept.

. . . . .

BACKSTAGE. CURTAIN UP: THIRTY MINUTES.

I am peeking through the curtains at the side of the stage to see the audience filing in. I see Mia at the theater door, surrounded by a group of friends including the girl from the coffee shop. Mr. Handsome has his hand on the small of her back, a girl is clasping her arm. And Mia is talking animatedly. She seems different. She tips her head back, laughing, I think, and there is that pain in my chest. Humiliation! Tonight it seems clearer than ever: I'm a tiny part of her life. I see only a piece of who she is. So much exists just in my head, and I know that, but tonight of all nights it hurts to remember. She has her own set of approvals to seek, and they have nothing to do with me. I close my eyes, trying to shake the painful embarrassment that starts in my stomach and wells up through my chest to my face. *Come on, Phyre. Forget about her.* There, up at the lighting board, I see you. My embarrassment eases and I draw back, staring instead at the set of the Price house behind the curtain and concentrating on what comes next: Lily.

. . . . .

DRESSING ROOM. CURTAIN UP: TEN MINUTES.

Trying for a minute to regain my focus, I sit alone at the mirror. You appear behind me.

YOU

Hey, you okay?

ME

Tip-top.

My heart is going a mile a minute with nerves. These last ten minutes are killing me. You smile.

YOU

Almost time.

ME

Almost.

YOU

I came to say break a leg. You got my note?

ME

Your note?

YOU

Yeah. With the flowers?

. . .

ME

Right. Yes!

How many times, Phyre! How many times can you make the same mistake? I have a moment of perfect clarity, and meet your eyes.

ME

You're the best. Thanks for everything.

YOU

Well. See you out there.

You smile one last time and close the door quietly behind you. I rub my hand across my forehead. I'm an idiot. *You're* the one that cares, not Mia, and this time I won't forget.

I hear the music start onstage and try to focus. This is it, the real thing, my chance to prove myself. Excitement claws at my throat as I make my way backstage.

. . . . .

BACKSTAGE. CURTAIN UP: THREE MINUTES.

Standing silently in the semidarkness, with only the slits of light between the curtains to show me the way, I take a few paces to relax, and bump into a figure coming toward me. Even in the dark, I know it's Mia. She squeezes both my hands in hers and puts her cheek against mine. Pressed to her, I remind myself again and again that we're not the only two people in the world. She whispers something to me but the music has picked up and her voice was too quiet to hear. I think of pulling her back to say *pardon* but she puts me at arm's length, her eyes catching the light for a second, and then she disappears through the curtain. She's gone. And she's not what's important.

. . . . .

THE CURTAIN RISES.

Lights up. The buzz is incredible, the excitement, the nerves, and the feeling of focus on one point in space. Light surrounded by darkness. I am Lily, dancing to the music and getting ready for my date with the man of my dreams.

The first half of the play sails by. I follow Gabe offstage to a bustle of excitement as the houselights come up. Cast members stop in at the dressing room to say how well it's going. I can hear through the speaker system the clangs of the set being changed and the floor of the Price house being taken up. As soon as I'm in my dress for the second half, I come out to have a look. Through the backstage curtains I can see the dark shape of the pool and there you are, wrapping silk greenery around the balcony rail. I think I catch a wink. When the curtain opens minutes later, I hear audible murmurs of appreciation from the audience as they notice the swimming pool. I can't wait to leap back into Lily's world, a world that feels so much more real and comfortable tonight than my own.

. . . . .

THE COUNTRY HOUSE OF PENNY FOSTER. EVENING.

Lily stands on the balcony overlooking a swimming pool. She gazes into the glistening blue water. Light glows through the windows of the house. A party is going on inside. There are voices and the clink of glasses. Bobby comes through the French window behind her. He hands her a soda bottle, then tugs at his suit sleeves and smooths his hair nervously.

BOBBY

Well, cheers.

LILY

Cheers!

Lily bubbles over.

Bobby! How did you get us in here? I can't believe you know these people.

BOBBY

I do have friends.

LILY

I see that. These girls would never have invited me.

BOBBY

I said I'd bring you out for a good time. And that's what I'm gonna do.

He glances inside.

You might not wanna go in. Your friend Michael is there.

LILY

Michael!

She scoffs unconvincingly.

I'm with you.

BOBBY

And you look beautiful.

At that moment, Michael comes onto the balcony with a girl. Lily quickly turns away from him toward the water. Flirting with the girl, Michael moves to put his arm around her when he sees Lily.

MICHAEL

Lily! You're here! I didn't know you knew Penny.

LILY

We have friends in common.

MICHAEL

Well, it's good to see you. Hey, I'm sorry I didn't make it the other night. The craziest thing happened and I tried to reach you.

The girl still stands beside him, hands on her hips. He is looking at Lily.

Can I get you a drink?

The girl rolls her eyes and stalks back inside, an insult echoing behind her.

I think she likes me!

Lily refuses to smile.

So. Can I call you?

She bites her lip.

LILY

Better if you don't.

Bobby steps up and takes Lily's hand.

BOBBY

Ready for that dance?

Michael raises his hands in mock surrender. He looks at Lily one last time before reluctantly going back into the house. Lily lets go of Bobby's hand, clapping hers together in satisfaction.

LILY

Ha. Did you see that! I turned him down and he walked away. That was amazing. Thanks. I owe you.

Bobby tries to hide his disappointment.

BOBBY

Sure, any time... Listen, I'm gonna grab another drink.

He gulps the rest of his drink and heads back inside. A figure has been watching from the doorway. She comes forward, a glamorous girl in a narrow-waisted polka-dot dress, seventeen, like Lily.

PENNY

What's your name?

LILY

Lily. I came with Bobby. You do know him, right?

PENNY

Of course. He does everything for us around here.

She looks carefully at Lily.

I'm Penny. I live here.

LILY

Right.

Penny leans against the balustrade, looking down into the pool.

PENNY

Lily. He's mentioned you.

LILY

He has?

PENNY

Do you like him?

LILY

Sure. He works for us too.

Penny looks unimpressed.

Oh, I'm not his girlfriend.

PENNY

I know that. But he likes you.

Penny tries to hide her jealousy. After an awkward silence, Bobby comes back out onto the balcony.

BOBBY

Penny! This is Lily, the one I told you about.

He is beaming with pride to be with her. Penny smiles politely.

PENNY

We've met.

Lily looks over at him, in his suit, with his hair smooth and the anxious furrow in his brow that she has started to see only recently. She has a pang of fondness for him. Penny excuses herself, leaving them alone, and is swallowed by the merriment of the house. The lights dim.

When the lights come up, time has passed. Lily and Bobby sit together beside the pool, beneath a lantern hanging from the balcony. The buzz of voices inside the house is louder. He has just found cause to reach for her hand when there is a clamor from inside and Michael stumbles through the French window. He has had too much to drink.

MICHAEL

There's my girl.

He moves toward Lily, and Bobby steps between them.

BOBBY

She's not *your* anything.

Michael ignores him, holding his hands up toward Lily's face.

MICHAEL

Lovely Lily!

Penny and her friends have appeared in the doorway.

BOBBY

That's enough. Leave her alone.

Michael turns on Bobby.

MICHAEL

Who says?

BOBBY

Me.

MICHAEL

And who are you to tell me what to do?

LILY

Stop it!

Michael swings at Bobby. Bobby steps back, narrowly avoiding the punch. He lunges at Michael in retaliation. They stumble backward, catching Lily in the fray. With the sudden commotion and the shouts that follow, no one sees her grab for something to regain her balance, find nothing, and tip into the water.

. . . . .

I hit the water hard, barely taking a breath before going under. Remembering that there's only four feet beneath me, I level out and feel the bottom of the tank against my palms. Opening my eyes, I override my instinct to swim to the surface and, trying not to cause a ripple, I swim along the floor of the tank where I can't be seen. My dress is fanning out around me and getting heavier as it takes in water. I look up at the lights on the surface—shimmering yellow orbs that make the blue of the water look green. I can see the dark shapes of the boys still tussling, the shouts strangely muted in this tranquil world. The pool stretches across the middle of the stage and appears to stop where it's covered by a lid at one end but the tank continues beneath the lid and into the wings where it opens again. Above me, blurry, I see the fake edge, and swim as smoothly as I can beneath it, lungs bursting, into the hidden part of the tank. Surfacing on the other side of the curtain, I take a silent gasp of air. The chants of *Fight, fight* onstage burst back into my consciousness, and I can already hear the murmurs of the audience wondering why I haven't resurfaced. Lily has hit her head on the bottom of the pool and with everyone's attention on the fight, no one has noticed. I push the wet hair away from my face and watch the stage.

Kate grabs Gabe's arm, Zach on his knees, his shirt torn, raising his hands above his head. Gabe holds his jaw and looks through the crowd for me. Not finding me, he goes toward the house but Kate is at the edge of the pool. More people start to assemble alongside it. She calls out, pointing frantically into the water. Gabe pulls off his jacket, kicks off his shoes, and jumps in. When I hear him hit the water, I take a breath and swim back into the tank.

We meet under water. He smiles, his skin pale in the blue light, his white shirt clinging. It feels like slow motion. He reaches for me, puts his arms under mine, and pulls me up. We burst through the surface of the water.

. . . . . .

Lily gasps for air, spluttering. Bobby rolls her up and onto the side of the pool, and climbs out beside her. Kneeling down, he wipes her wet hair away from her face. She opens her eyes and everyone crowds forward but Bobby puts up his hands.

BOBBY

Give her some space!

LILY

Bobby?

After a few moments, people start to retreat inside and there is quiet. Lily slowly props herself up on her elbows. She puts her hand to her head. Bobby, still dripping, smiles at her.

BOBBY

When I said I'd have you home by midnight, I pictured you alive.

She reaches for him and wraps her arms around his neck, still struggling to clear her throat.

LILY

Let's go home.

A few lights inside the house go off. The glistening surface of the water lies still. Bobby puts his jacket around her shoulders and picks her up. Blackout.

▪ ▪ ▪ ▪ ▪

DRESSING ROOM. FIVE MINUTES LATER.

Wet hair, clothes clinging to me, I stand in front of Mia. She reaches out and hugs me even though I'm soaking. I am very much me again. I hope I'll remember exactly how this feels when it's over. She holds my shoulders and puts me at arm's length, patches of damp left across her chest and arms.

MIA

You were brilliant. Even better than I
could have hoped.

There's a knock at the door and it's you. There are voices beyond you but you squeeze through and close it behind you. Your smile is intense.

YOU

Phy!

That's all, just "Phy," and it's better than a million words. You hug me. With you, I forget that my clothes are still wet. You're the first to step away and we're still smiling when I notice Mia moving toward the door. I turn to tell her to stay but she gives me a final nod of approval and, with a farewell wave, I watch her go. Mom appears in her place. She looks at me with new pride in her eyes. *See you at home, my star,* she says as she leaves. Cara's face is the next to appear.

CARA

F-ing genius! You can be in my movie any day.

She sends me a kiss and you follow her out. Elated, I change out of my wet clothes. I have this sense of achievement that I've never had before. I'm warm and dry-except for my hair, eyes still pink and hazy from the mixture of water and makeup—when you reappear. You're sitting by the mirror, talking about the effect the swimming-pool scene had, and behind you again is Mia. She beckons me to her.

MIA

I want to show you something.

I swing on my coat and follow her backstage. She pulls the curtain open a crack. There at the edge of the stage is a crowd of fifth graders, craning to see into the pool. *"How did she do it?" "She held her breath." "I could do it."* Pleased, I draw back through the curtain and Mia smiles. She tugs my coat around me in the dim light and begins to button it, saying something about staying warm with my hair wet but I'm watching her hands and I don't fully hear.

MIA

Are you ready to head out? Shall we walk?

You appear from the dressing room and I gesture for you to follow us. You shake your head.

YOU

Go ahead. I'll see you later.

I falter but Mia has already started toward the foyer so I skip to catch up.

▪ ▪ ▪ ▪ ▪

THEATER COURTYARD. SOON AFTER.

Together in the darkness, Mia and I cross toward the main school building. It's a fresh clear night but I don't feel the cold. My heart is warm. Time spent in darkness feels like a dream, like it might not have happened at all. Mia pulls her coat tighter around her, the silhouette I can recognize a mile away. She's leaving at the end of the semester. I wonder how clearly I'll be able to picture her face when she's gone. Tonight, the feeling doesn't fill me with concern. Something has changed this evening and right now I can't tell if it's resignation or if I'm just not scared to think of a world without Mia anymore. We cut through school and head into the warmth. Light breaks the mood of the darkness, washing out the shadows. As I'm wondering who I'll look out for each day, I see your reflection in the glass door as it closes. I turn, pleased.

ME

Hey. I thought you'd gone home.

YOU

Not yet.

MIA

I can drive you if you like.

I look from Mia to you.

ME

No, it's okay.

I wait for your confirming nod.

We'll walk.

We step out into the courtyard again, just the two of us. I glance back. Mia waves from the glowing window. She looks tiny surrounded by darkness. I stop to pull on my hat to keep out the chilly night air. You step in front of me and knot my scarf around my neck, reminding me of how Mia just buttoned my coat. You coax the scarf up around my face before walking on without a word. It felt nice. My expression changes but just for a second and I hope it's too dark for you to see.

. . . . .

MY KITCHEN. THE NEXT WEEK. MORNIING.

First day of vacation. I slept in. I'm still trying to adjust to the idea of free days, never seeing Mia again, and the end of the play. The phone rings and it's you. We talk, me sitting cross-legged and recalling, as I look out the window, that Mia could still someday show up expectedly.

YOU

How are you? I thought you might need cheering up.

ME

So did I!

Maybe you can hear the relief in my voice. And the surprise.

But I'm okay.

And I really mean it. There's a pause at your end, and when you speak again, you sound cheered.

YOU

Great. I'm really glad. That's great. So, maybe we could get together soon.

ME

Sure. Sounds *great.*

You pretend to laugh and then you really are laughing. You say "great" once more for luck before hanging up the phone.

. . . . .

MY FRONT DOORSTEP. SOON AFTER.

I'm picking up the mail when I see a shape through the frosted diamond of stained glass in the entranceway. The doorbell rings and there's a distorted you. I falter. I wasn't expecting you so soon. When you said "get together" I didn't realize you meant right now. I feel something like happiness and self-consciousness—I'm still not dressed—rolled into one. I open the door.

ME

Hi. I didn't know you were coming.

Your smile flickers.

YOU

Sorry. I guess I should have been clearer.

ME

No harm done.

I tug my T-shirt down awkwardly and step aside. You follow me in.

. . . . .

MY BEDROOM. SOON AFTER.

I sweep some clothes off my bed, then sit down and tuck my knees up under my chin. You sit beside me, strangely far away—as far as the furniture will allow. Still trying to compensate for my surprise at your arrival, I salute cheerfully.

ME

Ahoy there, matey.

No smile.

Is something wrong?

You shake your head but your eyes say otherwise.

YOU

Phyre . . .

You never use my name like that! Something's definitely up.

. . . I'm glad to have you back.

I keep quiet in case you're going to go on. Now that Mia's gone? I shift, embarrassed.

ME

I never really went away.

I'm lying, I know, and you're still looking at the floor. I give you another minute and still you don't speak.

ME

What is it? Have I done something?

You're shaking your head and with sudden exasperation you stand.

YOU

I give up.

Now I'm really confused.

ME

What do you mean?

You're more intense than I've ever seen you.

YOU

I keep . . . for some reason, thinking that . . . you finally get it. And every time, you make it really clear that you don't!

You fix me with a stare and see that I'm as confused as ever.

You still don't know?

ME

Know what?

YOU

God, Phyre, you can be so stupid. All you see is Mia, Mia, Mia.

You're at the door.

And all I see is you.

. . .

. . .

. . .

We're silent. I . . .

For the first time, you almost smile. Ruefully.

YOU

I'm pretty sure I don't want to be you. And that can only mean I want to kiss you.

. . .

ME

. . . You . . . never said!

YOU

I tried.

I see you standing there, so much older than in my head.

And then what?

ME

Well, I could have . . . have . . .

I fade out. You say something else, that this is what you were afraid of. And when I look up—

You're gone.

Since that conversation—one week, five days, and three hours. I've called you every day. You haven't called me back. I can see it now. You were always there, every time I needed you. I can't help wondering if you felt as invisible as I did with Mia, but I can't know if you won't talk to me . . .

▪ ▪ ▪ ▪ ▪

THE STREET. EVENING.

The sky is dark and heavy but my mind is made up. I'm not even out the door when the rain comes, torrential rain, splashing up from the sidewalk so that my legs are as wet as my arms. The pavement glistens. I start to run, pushing my slick hair away from my face. I think of the last time I ran toward you, my eyes closed on the playing field that day. And suddenly it feels like I've been running toward you with my eyes closed for the past three months. I can feel the rain dripping down my neck but I don't stop to put my collar up. I round the corner, relieved to see the lights on at your house up ahead. In a second I'm on your doorstep, bedraggled, soaked to the skin. If you looked through the peephole now, you'd see me. Come and answer the bell. Please! There's no use taking shelter now, so I step back and let the rain pour down my face. I think I see the upstairs curtain move. Then, as I stand here, as quickly as the rain started, it tapers to slow thick drops, and then stops. I look up at the clearing sky, suddenly aware of how I must look. Being wet in the rain is romantic; being wet when it's not raining is poor planning, and now I feel stupid. The porch light comes on and I squint at its brightness. You pull open the door.

ME

Hi.

YOU

Hi.

You give me the look that I know is reserved for me, the only-you look. Then, instead of inviting me in, you step out to join me. Standing on the top step in the mist of moisture left in the air, you look at me. I don't wait for you to say anything else. I kiss you, my arms wrapped tightly around your waist and I pull you toward me so I feel the full length of your body. Kissing you is amazing. It's right. Still half a step down I look into your eyes.

You smile.

▪ ▪ ▪ ▪ ▪ ▪

FADE OUT.

Acknowledgments

I would love to thank Chandra Wohleber of the red pen, Alexei Esikoff of the green pen, Caroline Abbey, and all the amazing people at Bloomsbury.